CHARLOTTE'S WEBSITE

OTHER BOOKS BY LINDA M. AU

MORE RED INK MYSTERIES

The Scarlet Letter Opener (Red Ink Mystery #1)
The Tell-Tale Heart Attack (Red Ink Mystery #2)

Other Novels:

Secret Agent Manny
Gray Area

Humor/Essays:

Head in the Sand . . . and other unpopular positions
Fork in the Road . . . and other pointless discussions
Train of Thought: Travel Essays from a One-Track Mind
Travel Documents

another red ink mystery

CHARLOTTE'S WEBSITE

Linda M. Au

vicious circle publishing

Copyright © 2020 by Linda M. Au
Vicious Circle Publishing

Charlotte's Website (Red Ink Mystery #3)

ISBN: 978-1-954973-01-5

Cover artwork by Mike Ferrin (mikeferrin.org)

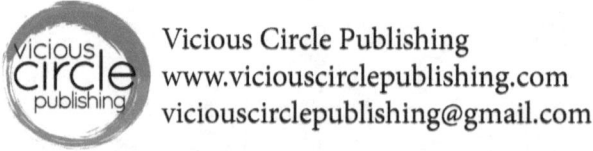

Vicious Circle Publishing
www.viciouscirclepublishing.com
viciouscirclepublishing@gmail.com

For Fara
She knows why

and for Suzy
She knows why, too

Chapter 1

NO, I THINK IT'S REALLY GOOD. BETTER AND BETTER."

"Really, Maggie? It's good?"

"Charlotte, I wouldn't kid about this. And I wouldn't fib, either. Yes, I think it's in good shape and I think it has a lot of potential. As usual."

"Then why the hesitation?"

"Well..."

She'd caught me. The problem wasn't her writing style. That was always interesting and beautiful in its own way. It wasn't her grammar or spelling—something I, as her proofreader, would have had no trouble telling her as part of my work for her. It was something else—something I didn't feel qualified to comment on because she wrote in a genre that I never read. Ever. On purpose.

"I knew it! You don't like it! You think it sucks!"

I waved my hands and shook my head. "No, seriously, it's not that. Your writing is always top notch."

"Then what?" she asked and bit her lip, a sure sign that she was feeling insecure. And I was sure she had no reason to feel this way, that the issue was mine and not hers. But, how to tell her this?

"Charlotte, listen. You know the old 'It's not you. It's me' line? Well, that's what's going on here. YOU are not the problem. But I just don't feel comfortable reading this stuff from you because it's not my favorite genre."

"Not your favorite?"

"Not... at all."

"Meaning?"

"Meaning I don't ever read fantasy horror bondage stuff, or *whatever* this is. I don't even really know."

"It's dark fantasy."

"Okay."

"With a little horror and bondage thrown in."

"Okayyyy..."

"And some sadistic—"

"*Not* okay. See, that's where you completely lose me. Up until then I could at least play along and just tell myself that it wasn't my cup of tea. But once you start crossing that line, then—"

"What line, exactly?"

"Oh, I think you know what line."

She shrugged. "Yeah, I know what line."

"So, don't take it personally. Your manuscript is in good shape. The proofreading went smoothly, as it always does. Your grammar is good. Your sentence structure is marvelous. Your storytelling abilities are through the roof. It's just the *story* you're telling isn't the kind I would normally read."

"Normally read?"

"Not... at all."

"Fair enough. Different strokes then, to coin a phrase."

I remembered the scene with a bit of S&M lashing and smirked at her use of "different strokes."

"So, you're not mad? Because your readers will love this. It's ready."

She smiled. "My editor loved it, so I was hoping you'd get through it easily. No fact-checking issues then, either?"

"Not much in the way of fact checking on this one, since you made up a lot of your own rules... again. It won't take you all that long to get through the corrections and then you'll be all set."

"Good. Email me the document and I'll get through those corrections so my editor can have this back on time for a change."

Charlotte sipped her tea and smiled over her cup. I reached across the table and patted her hand reassuringly. She may have been a fairly successful novelist, but she was only in her late thirties and still needed some reassurance that she was actually good at this writing thing. She suffered from Impostor Syndrome more than most writers I worked with. Heck, I suffered from it myself as a proofreader, thinking I was always just faking it and making up my own grammar rules as I went along. It was why I consulted the *Chicago Manual of Style* a hundred times a day while I was working: I never quite trusted myself to know what I was doing. I had to guess that a writer—specifically a fiction writer—had to suffer from it far worse than I. She smiled again.

"Seriously, Charlotte, nobody writes this stuff as well as you do. Nobody."

"Do you even *know* anybody who writes this stuff besides me?"

"Well, no."

We both burst out laughing and drank the rest of our lovely hot beverages in contented silence. Proofreader gone for the day. Friend and ally stepping in. It was turning out to be a good day after all.

I CAME HOME FROM MY COFFEE and lunch meeting with Charlotte to find my obnoxious little dog, Vlad, cowering in a corner of the kitchen. That usually meant one of two things, and they were both bad. He had either chewed something to bits or he had peed somewhere he shouldn't have. After taking him outside to do his doggy business, I stepped gingerly into the kitchen, on the lookout for stray puddles, and found none. So it was likely a chewing incident. A quick glance at the couch showed a throw pillow that Vlad had tortured and killed for me, apparently thinking it dangerous in some way only a small dog left alone for hours would understand. I sighed, looked at the guilt-ridden Vlad, and said nothing. He had probably been torturing himself for his misdeed for the past few hours while he waited for me to return and scold him. I just wasn't up for any dog shaming right now.

"You're off the hook, you little weasel," I said to him crossly as I left the kitchen and headed down the hall toward the bathroom. Time to slip into comfy sweats and settle in for the rest of the day and evening. The work of proofreading Charlotte's dark horror novel wasn't taxing work. But reading that much gory detail and disturbing material—well, it was disturbing for *me*, anyway—drained me more than actual work. Punctuation issues or grammar glitches didn't wear me out. In fact, I was one of those sick grammar nazis who got a strange thrill out of noticing other people's mistakes. It was part of why I could command such good freelance rates and make a living at my nitpicking. So, it was only the material itself in this case that had me feeling worn out and weary before I had even gotten myself dinner. Vlad's little escapade with my throw pillow was vexing, but I was already too far gone to care about it enough to chastise him properly.

Once I was in sweats, I padded back out to the living room to more properly survey the damage to the pillow. At least he had been gracious enough to choose a throw pillow I wasn't fond of. If he had chewed the one my mom had gotten me—the one with the squirrel embroidered on it—he would have gotten a bit of a thrashing. Well, as much as one can thrash a small dog who'd likely be shivering and cowering and looking adorable in an attempt to avoid punishment. I picked up the dead pillow, its guts hanging out in loose threads, still damp in spots where he had gotten doggy saliva all over it. He had evidently enjoyed his life of crime while I was away, and I tossed the ravished pillow onto the floor at my feet and sat down on the couch. Vlad came up to me and looked first at the shredded pillow in front of him and then up at me on the couch. He was weighing the pros and cons of joining me. Normally he was quite welcome up here and didn't hesitate to hoist his little self up onto the couch.

But staring at that pillow he had mangled, I could almost read his thoughts. *Is she mad at me? Do I dare jump up there as if nothing has happened? Did she put this here to warn me? to scold me? to shame me? I wonder if there's any food left in the bowl...*

He stood there by the couch and started to shiver from sheer nervousness. Poor thing. I took pity on him—after all, I'd had a rough day too so I could empathize—and patted the couch cushion next to me. Vlad immediately launched himself up onto the couch and curled up next to me, his entire back end wiggling with delight at having avoided what he must have assumed would be an inevitable chiding from Mama.

"There you go, you crazy little dog. Just don't try it with any of the other pillows next time I'm away from home, or you'll be looking for another forever home."

He didn't speak English very well, of course, so he just kept wagging his tail and licking my face in glee, fully enjoying his reprieve. And, of course, it was just the sort of pick-me-up I needed today. I turned on the television with the remote and searched for something mindless and light to give me back my emotional equilibrium. I was glad it typically took Charlotte two years to finish a novel in that genre, because I was sure I couldn't handle that much dark horror (or dark fantasy or whatever) any more frequently than that. Even if she was a really good speller.

Chapter 2

SO ANYWAY, MAGGIE, I WAS JUST SAYING TO JOANNE that I thought you were working on the new book from Charlotte. Yes? Please tell me yes!"

"Geez, Helga, calm down! It's just a book." I grinned at her as innocently as I could.

"But you know I love her books."

"Of course you do. Somebody's buying those things, and it sure isn't me."

She laughed. "Maggie, I tell ya, you don't know what you're missing."

"Apparently I do. I read them before anyone else, remember? I'm the proofreader."

"True. But you read it for errors. Do you honestly pay enough attention that you know what you're reading?"

I shook my head. I'd had work associations with Helga for many years because I proofed the local newspaper and she was the receptionist and secretary there. I would have thought that she'd have a good idea about what I did by now, but I guess unless someone watches me work or has been on the receiving end of my proofreading, she might not know how much I do have to pay attention as I read.

"Of course I have to pay attention. How else would I be able to correct broader sentence structure or do any sort of basic fact checking at all?"

"Fair, chickie, fair enough. Still... it can't be the same as curling up with a good book in the recliner and enjoying it that way. You know, without having to pay attention to whether somebody is using that Oxford comma you seem to be so fond of."

I could always count on Helga to spice up a conversation and get right to the point.

"Well, maybe not. But it's a lot closer than you think. I have a bad habit of noticing mistakes in printed books that have supposedly been through a proofreader already, even if I think I'm reading them for pleasure."

"I bet you proofread the news crawl at the bottom of the TV screen when you're watching the news too, don't you?"

"Guilty as charged."

"You're just a complete barrel of laughs all the time, ain't you, missy?"

I chuckled and grabbed the envelope off the counter. "Oh yes, I'm the life of the party. But you already knew that, didn't you?"

"Is this answer-a-question-with-another-question day or what?"

"Ha, I see what you did there!"

"I just love when you come down to the paper, chickie. Haven't seen you much lately since that nasty business with Frank."

She frowned and pursed her lips, almost willing herself to not say anything else. I sighed.

"Let's not go there, all right? I think we all need to forget that whole escapade."

Helga was referring to my now ex-boyfriend, Frank. I had a feeling I wasn't ready for another relationship after my divorce, even if it had been nearly five years ago now. Some things just needed time to heal, and apparently I was one of them. Still, the relationship with Frank had been fun while it lasted.

"Oops, sorry. Didn't realize that was still a sore spot."

"You can guess why that is, I'm sure. Anyway, let's just pretend that never happened. Deal?"

She thrust her hand across the counter. "Deal." I shook it and nodded. Solidarity between friends. That's what it was all about sometimes. And if anyone could rally behind a woman in distress over a man, it was Helga. She wasn't overly fond of anyone with a Y chromosome. Someday I'd have to ask her exactly why that was. There had to be quite a story there that she'd never told me. A nice lunch and a few glasses of chardonnay and she'd probably be more than willing to tell me all about it. I'd just be worried that Helga's story would remind me too much of Charlotte's novels. Maybe I'd need a few glasses of that chardonnay myself so I could hear her story properly.

CHARLOTTE COLLINS WAS GENERALLY A CHEERFUL, happy woman, despite the reputation her chosen book genre may have given her to some of her fans. Those of us who knew her in person, who lived here in Brighton with her, usually treated her as one of our own, without doing any sort of fangirling or other stalker activity that so often comes with success. She'd found that success five novels ago with her first book, and it had been a heady roller coaster ride for Charlotte ever since. I'd been her proofreader since those early days when she needed to prep that first finished manuscript to send off to possible agents. I knew then that she had a gift for writing, even if it wasn't the sort of story I would typically read. I'd learned how to discern the former talent not based on the latter choice of topic a long time ago. And although I usually bowed out of offering my personal opinion on the worthiness of a client's writing, I'd always jumped at the chance to assure Charlotte that her writing was indeed publishable. Even in those early days before she'd snagged her current agent.

Since then she had kept me on as her manuscript proofreader

so that she was sending in the best possible version of her work every time. I was happy to oblige, and with the last two books, her publisher had let me proofread the final layout as well. They usually hired freelancers anyway, so it wasn't much of a stretch for Charlotte to voice an opinion about which proofreader they used for her books. Not by that point, when she was commanding spots on best-seller lists and had become one of their top-notch authors. They weren't a huge press to begin with, and I continued to give Charlotte and her publisher my lower "friend" rate for proofreading, so the working relationship was a win-win for everyone.

Charlotte, though, wasn't as tech savvy as her publisher would have liked. Some of their other authors were maintaining their own author sites, with hot links to the publisher's site and lots of other connections to the mothership. But Charlotte had trouble handling even a basic blog page on her site, so Seth helped her out a little in the beginning. Seth, my grown son, dabbled in all things web-coding-geek and initially helped Charlotte out at my request when she was struggling through the final edits of that first novel. The publisher insisted that she start and maintain an author site, so Seth helped her throw together something she could update on her own, using a template and a simple interface to write a blog entry every now and then. She loved to write, loved to update her blog, but wrung her hands over the not-too-complicated technical process involved in getting the website to update properly. I'd been online for many years—since Seth was a young boy, actually—and so I found her frustration almost comical and quaint.

One morning not long after I had handed back her proofread manuscript via email, I got a frantic call from Charlotte. I heard her son Teddy whining in the background. He was nine and long past the age when whining could be considered cute or even tolerable. But it was Saturday, and raining, and dreary, so Teddy was probably bored to tears and driving his mother nuts being stuck inside all day.

"Hi, Charlotte!" I said, trying to sound chipper and upbeat and hoping she'd catch the enthusiasm. "What can I do for you?"

She sighed loudly. "There's something wrong with my website."

I sighed in return, but not for the same reason. I hadn't gotten a call like this from Charlotte in quite some time, not since the early days of her website when everything was new to her and it was all a bit much for her to take in and remember. But she had been running the site and blog for several years now and, for the most part, things had been going smoothly. I was secretly hoping that this didn't signal the beginning of another period of hand holding between Charlotte and either me or Seth. Or both.

"What happened?" I was secretly hoping she had just forgotten her password or something else easy to fix. I was also hoping she would be able to articulate it clearly enough for me to understand the problem, in case I had to be called in to fix it or to explain it to Seth so he could fix it.

"I think somebody's hacked into my website, Maggie."

"But you're not sure?"

"Well, no. Not exactly."

"Why not?" I was beginning to fear the worst: that Charlotte and I weren't speaking the same language.

"Because I don't exactly know what a hacked website looks like."

Fair enough, I thought, though I also realized that this wasn't going to be all that straightforward.

"Well, it can look like any number of things. Are you noticing changes on the site itself, or in the dashboard where you write your blog entries?"

"Yes."

"Yes?" I asked, already worried that this was now going to eat up the rest of my afternoon.

"I mean... no?"

I laughed. It was funny, albeit frustrating. "Which one is it?"

"I don't know!"

"Well, what's making you think it was hacked? What looks different?"

"Are you near a computer?"

"I'm always near a computer."

She chuckled. "Well, go to my website and tell me what you see."

I opened a browser and typed in her URL. It auto-filled after a few characters and I was soon on her site. What greeted me didn't initially look any different from her usual macabre black background with strange iridescent lettering and odd, eerie icons and drawings, plus the covers of all of her books in a row along the top of the page. Then I saw it. There were a bunch of skulls and crossbones along the top, under the book cover images, and each one was animated, laughing in a skinless, fleshless grin, with the words "SOMEONE WILL DIE!" flashing underneath each image in gaudy fluorescent green lettering.

"Oh, shit!" I said.

"Ah, so you see it too, then."

"You bet I do. Holy crap, Charlotte. Is this a teaser for the new book?"

"No! What am I supposed to do about this?"

"Offhand, I don't know. But we can start by disabling the site until I can get Seth to take a look at it."

I walked her through the couple of clicks needed to temporarily put the site offline. Visitors would get a somewhat generic error message—with an apology—if they tried to go to the site. Not ideal, but better than the skull and crossbones bit and whatever it carried with it.

"Thanks, Maggie. That wasn't too hard after all."

"No, but it doesn't solve your problem. We still need to figure out what's going on and how to stop it. But for now, at least your readers won't click through to anything nasty."

"That's my main concern, too. It'd be awful to hear that someone got a computer virus or something just because they were trying to buy one of my books."

"Speaking of clicking through, do you know how many hits your site gets on any given day? Like, how many people may have been to your site since those skulls showed up?"

"More than I'm comfortable, with, I can tell you, Maggie. Do you want me to figure that out?"

"No, I was just asking out of curiosity."

"Well, it may have been more than usual, the past few days..."

Her voice trailed off a little. I could sense the uncomfortable tone in her voice.

"Why? What's wrong?"

"I may have just put up a few teasers about the new book on Monday."

"You didn't."

"Yeah, I did. The publisher encouraged me, and I put up three or four tiny excerpts from the opening scenes."

"You didn't," I repeated, sighing.

"I did. That always drives traffic to the site like crazy."

"Uh huh."

"That's *usually* a good thing."

"Usually." I laughed, deciding to find this funny instead of frustrating.

"Oh, good," Charlotte replied, clearly relieved. "So you're not mad at me then, Maggie?"

"Why would I be mad at you?"

"Well, the site's probably getting twice the traffic it would have gotten last week. Twice as many opportunities for something bad to happen to one of my readers."

"That's not your fault, Charlotte. It's just bad timing. Or maybe whoever did this was waiting for a time when the site would get a lot more traffic. In which case, then it would have happened at some point later, if not now. Maybe when this book came out and you'd have advertised it on your site then."

"I hadn't thought of it that way. You're probably right."

"Anyway, we've taken care of it for now. I'll let you know what Seth says about what to do next. But at least we won't be harming anyone else."

"Again, Charlotte, I can't thank you enough."

We hung up, and I clicked off her website and thought about burying my nose in the next project, a theological tome from a seminary student. Ugh. Maybe her dark horror wasn't so bad after all. Time to call Seth.

Chapter 3

MOM, I JUST DON'T SEE WHY YOU expose yourself to this stuff."

Annie was home from college—her senior year, finally—and sat across from me at my small kitchen table in the second-floor apartment I shared with Vlad the Inhaler. He was sniffing around the floor at her feet, clearly remembering her high school days of carelessly dropping crumbs and bits of food from her plate onto the floor. She'd learned a few lessons in tidiness since then, though, now that she was out on her own and had to clean up her own floors. Vlad gave up and sat down under her chair, curling up his little Cairn terrier self and huffing his frustration through his wet, cold nose.

"I'm not 'exposing' myself to anything, Annie. It's my job."

"You're a freelancer for a reason, Mom. You can say no to any client you want."

"I'm a freelancer so I can sleep in in the mornings and so I can wear sweats all day long. But I get your point. I just don't agree with it."

"Why not? The stuff Charlotte writes is... disturbing."

"Yes, I know it's disturbing. Probably better than you do, since I have to read every word of it. I'm pretty sure you're not reading Charlotte's books in between rereadings of *Pride and Prejudice*."

"Mom..." She rolled her eyes, and I burst out laughing. It was strangely nice to see memories of the teenager she once was, complete with the drama and a little bit of the mom-embarrassment.

"What?" I asked, feigning confusion and a little of my own drama.

"Seriously. Don't read that stuff anymore."

"I'm going to keep reading it, Annie. Charlotte isn't just a client. She's a friend of mine, since before she was published. I helped her get her start. I'm not going to back out of that now."

"See what I mean? This is partly your fault. The world doesn't need stories like that."

"It needs more puppies and kittens then, right? Charlotte's stuff appeals to a certain group of people, and among that group she is selling ridiculously well. I'm... happy for her." I had to hesitate there. I wasn't at all sure I was happy for her. She could have used her writing talent in any number of genres. Why the dark horror fantasy stuff appealed to her as a writer still confused me. But this wasn't the time to admit that to Annie. There was a larger principle here.

"And that's what's wrong with the world!" Annie declared, standing up and waving her hands over her head in exasperation.

"Honey, if that's all that was wrong with the world, we'd be in pretty good shape, to be honest with you."

She frowned at me and headed for the refrigerator, where she took out one of my cans of Diet Coke and flipped the tab open.

Sitting back down at the table, she sipped some of the soda and then finally smiled at me.

"Okay then, other than all that, how is Charlotte doing? Pretty well, I guess, based on her popularity."

"She really is thriving as an author. It's gratifying to see her success. But she's only one of my clients."

"The newspaper? You still proofing for them?"

"Yup. Somehow they keep hanging in there with their

subscribers, but I can see already they're shifting heavily into the online paper instead. They have me proofreading more of the online stuff these days, so I assume they'll carry me along with their site as a freelancer, no matter how their future plays out."

"You mean, if the print edition dies?"

"Precisely. Kinda like radio stations, really. People are turning to more cloud and online options. Sucks for people like me who remember the purity and beauty of the simpler ways."

"People like you. You mean old people." She grinned, then took another big swig of the Diet Coke.

"Smart ass," I said, winking at her across the table. No matter how old she got, no matter how grown up and mature, she was still the younger child with the idealistic streak a mile wide. Now that she was a young woman, though, and not a drama-filled teenager, it was a refreshing personality trait and one I was oddly proud of. I sometimes wondered if I was far too pragmatic whenever Annie got onto one of her moral high horses. She had a way of making me feel bad about things I wouldn't normally have thought twice about. Most of the time I still thought she was oversimplifying too many things in the name of her moral high ground, but once in a while she struck a chord—or, more accurately, a nerve.

This wasn't one of those times. I drew a few lines in the sand with clients' content when I proofread, but Charlotte's books didn't cross that personal line. Sure, they were gory and detailed and perhaps a bit disturbing. But they didn't violate my personal ethics or my general worldview. She wasn't spouting anti-religious stuff or pro-Satan worship. Stuff like that. It was just... gross. Well, gross to me, at least. And to Annie.

"You haven't actually *read* any of her books, have you?" I asked her.

"Heck no. I wouldn't go near that entire genre!"

"I figured, but I thought I'd ask. You were sounding pretty sure of what's in them just now."

"Only by reputation. And the book covers. They're gross."

"So you *do* judge a book by its cover then!" I smiled.

"Everybody does. You know that. It's why all your clients spend more on their covers than they do on their proofreading."

"That's because I don't charge enough."

"Been saying that for years, Mom. You sell yourself short. Always have."

"Sweetie," I said, reaching across the table to place my hand on top of hers, "listen. I really appreciate your looking out for me and what I'm reading. And you know there are certain types of work I would never take on. It's just that this isn't one of them. Not only that, but Charlotte is my friend. I'd want to help her any way I can, unless she crossed that line with what she was writing. But she hasn't. And so, I'll keep helping her."

"I know," she sighed. "It's just... gross."

"Yes, so you said," I said and smiled at her. This was just going to have to be one of those things we agreed to disagree on. If this was the worst thing we disagreed on right now, I'd consider that a major victory with a twenty-two-year-old daughter.

"Other than all this then," she said, waving her hand as if dismissing our earlier, distasteful topic, "have you seen Seth much lately?"

"Ah, he's busy. You know how he is. Locks himself up in that apartment of his and works twelve hours a day and then plays video games the other twelve."

She smiled. "Glad to see he hasn't changed then. I can get him to email me sometimes, but usually it'll just be a text or something."

"Well, I could do without the constant video gaming, but he's Seth, after all. The video games kind of come with the territory."

"Is he back to playing baseball yet? You know, since the, well... since what happened last year?"

She was referring to the unfortunate murder of one of his baseball teammates late last summer. Seth had been there when Allen Joneston had died on the field, and Seth himself had been temporarily implicated in the murder because he'd brought the cooler of energy drinks that had apparently been poisoned. Well, that *one* bottle had been poisoned, anyway. Poor Allen.

"No, not really. The whole team took this year off."

"The whole team? How did I not hear about this till now?"

"Seth doesn't really like to talk about it, that's why. The team just figured their hearts weren't in it this year, so they all unanimously decided to quietly not sign up this year. It was the right decision."

"That's a shame. It was kind of the only real exercise Seth got."

"I know. And I liked that he'd made all those friends and was otherwise doing something social for a change. But trust me, it was the right choice for them, for the whole team. And Seth in particular. He didn't even go to any Pirates games."

"None?"

"Nope."

"Wow. Poor Seth. Maybe I'll give him a call later."

"No don't do that. He's really trying not to think about it. Don't bring it up. Besides, he'll be here for dinner later. So you'll get to see him then, in a more normal context. If he wants to talk about it, let's let him start the conversation, okay?"

"But he's okay otherwise?"

"You've seen him at breaks and holidays, sweetie. You know he's fine."

"Well, I'm asking you as his *mom*. I know quite well that sometimes moms get more information than little sisters. He'd probably tell you things he wouldn't tell me. And even if not, he would probably at least give off vibes to you that I wouldn't see or notice. Even if it's just because he lives near you and I'm away at school so much."

She had a point. The mom radar was a real thing, and a good mom could usually sense when something was "off" with one of her kids. Plus, Seth was always fairly easy to read, so whatever "vibe" Annie was referring to would have been doubly obvious with Seth. He had never been the silent, brooding type. A little introverted, sure, but not so much with his parents. And I had always had the sense that he was doing all right since the murder and its aftermath last year. The lack of baseball, an outlet for him—both physically and emotionally—was unfortunate, but it truly had been the right choice. And Seth had been instrumental in that decision. I had been proud of him at the time and was proud of him now, too. I had never second-guessed their choice to sit out this season in memory of poor Allen. Annie was simply behind the times on this one. And maybe once she talked to Seth tonight at dinner, she'd see for herself that Seth was healing as well as could be expected. It's not every day someone in your family gets accused of murder, after all. Well, not in most families, anyway.

"He's fine. You'll get to see for yourself in a few hours. Now, let's take poor Vlad for a walk. He's barely been outside all day today, and it's so gorgeous out there right now with the fall leaves."

"Good idea," Annie said, and off we went for a little mom-and-daughter (and dog) time.

DINNER WITH SETH AND ANNIE was uneventful, but still made my mother's heart swell with pride and happiness. It was getting rarer to find ways to get both of my now-adult children in the same room at the same time these days, and I feared that would only get harder as they got older. Annie wisely steered completely away from any talk of the baseball team or Allen's murder, and I was grateful to her for that. Seth seemed happy to see her, and always happy to eat whatever food I put in front of him. And, of course, Vlad was delighted to have both of his best buddies in the apartment with us. He was camped out under the table, eternally optimistic about his chances at food scraps falling to the floor, where they automatically became his. But Seth's days of purposely dropping broccoli and other yucky vegetables to the floor were long gone. Being out on his own had taught Seth the value of a home-cooked meal, and I obliged by feeding the kids some of their favorites when they came to visit.

"Pass the potatoes," Seth said, scarfing down the last bite of the pile he had already taken earlier. I grabbed the bowl and handed it to him.

"Here you go."

"That's a lot of potatoes," Annie chimed in.

"I'm a growing boy, Annie," he said, smirking at her and taking the bowl from me happily. "I need my carbohydrates."

"Uh huh. Right." She speared a bit of broccoli and rolled her eyes—again. It was apparently still her favorite exercise, and she had perfected it as an art form since age sixteen.

"So anyway, Seth," I interjected, "what do you think we can do for Charlotte and that website of hers?"

"I'll have to take a look at it myself to be sure. I won't know for sure what happened until I can get under the hood and take a closer look. Asking Charlotte what happened over the phone didn't get me anywhere."

I chuckled. "I know what you mean. She doesn't exactly speak the language, does she?"

"Speak the language? She doesn't even know what the language *is*, let alone speak it!"

"Not her fault, Seth. Be nice. Different skill set."

"Mom, *you* have more online skills than Charlotte does!"

I frowned. "What is *that* supposed to mean, exactly?"

Annie grinned. "He's trying to tell you that you're old, Mom."

"I've been online since before you were born, missy, so don't get all uppity on me about my computer skills."

Sometimes I loved that I could always pull that fact out of the air and wave it in Annie's face. I had gotten my first computer, an ancient Tandy 2000—back in the late eighties—years before Annie came along. I had been the reason both of them knew anything about computers in the first place.

She frowned. "I hate when you bring that up."

"Because it reminds you that you're still in diapers," said Seth through a mouthful of mashed potatoes.

"Hey!"

Seth and I both laughed.

"Anyway, Mom," Seth continued, "I'm not sure what to tell you about Charlotte's website until I see it for myself. I talked to her earlier today, and she didn't want to give me the password to get in and take a look around. I tried to explain to her how to create a temporary password so I could go in, and then she could change it back once I was done, but that made her nervous, for some reason."

"Why, for goodness' sake? It's just a temporary password."

He sighed. It seems we both had difficult clients who were vexing to deal with.

"I have no idea, but I gave up trying to explain it to her."

"Then how are we going to help her out? Whatever happened, someone needs to get into that site and undo everything, and maybe even figure out who did this and why. If it's something that can be prosecuted, I'm sure she'll want to see them punished. Her website being down is bad for business, and she knows that much about the internet, at least."

"So, tell me again," said Annie, reaching down to pat Vlad on the head, which only encouraged him and gave him a false sense of hope that he would indeed see a morsel tossed in his direction. "Why does a woman her age refuse to learn more about the internet than the bare basics?"

"I don't know, sweetie," I said. "She's only about ten years older than Seth. Old enough to have lived before the internet was ubiquitous, but definitely young enough to have embraced the digital age a lot more than she has."

"She's a Luddite," said Seth, concentrating on the meat loaf he had added to his plate. "Some people just don't like high-tech stuff. She's one of them."

"Doesn't it bother you, though?" Annie asked. "That she needs so much hand holding to do the simplest things?"

He grinned. "Hell no. Why would it bother me? How do you think I make a living? If everybody knew how to run their websites and design them, I'd be working at McDonald's."

"I suppose."

"Just like Mom is glad half the writers in the world still can't spell properly, even with spell-check. Somebody has to set them straight and tidy up their messes. Mom and I both sort of do that for them, only in different areas."

"So," Annie interjected, "you're saying that both you and Mom profit from the fact that we live in a fallen world."

"How so?"

"Well, in a perfect world, people wouldn't make these mistakes and both of you would be working at McDonald's."

"In a perfect world, honey," I said demurely, "there wouldn't *be* any McDonald's." I smiled.

"Mom, bite your tongue!" Seth said, and we all laughed. "Anyway, I'll be heading over to Charlotte's house tomorrow morning to sit at *her* computer with her there. She'll sign in to her website's dashboard and then will let me take a peek. That ought to be fun. I'm just hoping it's not too bad, whatever happened."

Chapter 4

THE KNOCKING AT THE DOOR was a lot more insistent than it should have been. I reminded myself that the new downstairs neighbors disliked keeping the main apartment building door locked except during a few scant hours overnight or when they were out of town, which then allowed anyone easy access to the inside hallway and staircase to the other two apartments. So, it literally could have been anybody pounding on my apartment door at eight thirty on a Saturday morning.

Whoever it was, they were about to hear a barrage of nasty words unfit for a sailor for awakening me at such an ungodly hour. It had to be either a cult missionary of some sort or the UPS delivery guy with something I had ordered and forgotten about. Either way, this was too early to be banging on my door. I swung my legs out of bed and stood—a little too quickly, as my head swam a bit and I had to grab the bedpost to keep myself from falling back onto the mattress. Another hour and I might have been prepared to meet the world. It was a difficult thing, being a night owl in a daytime world.

I was reaching for my bathrobe, which was at the foot of the bed, when the rumbling of an excited voice came down the hall to my bedroom, even through the closed door.

"Mom! It's me! Open up!"

It was Seth. And he sounded more than a little upset.

I dashed down the hallway and headed straight for the door, flinging it open in one sweep after turning the deadbolt. Seth stood in the hallway, panting and puffing as if he had just finished running a marathon.

"What? What, Seth?" I stood back from the doorway and flagged him inside with a wave of my hand, watching him shake as he stumbled inside and headed straight for the couch. Vlad, meanwhile, had accompanied me out from the bedroom and was dashing around Seth's feet, mistaking the excitement for the good kind that typically involved food or going outside for a walk. Seth plopped down onto the couch and Vlad was in his lap a second later, licking his face and otherwise making an adorable nuisance of himself.

"Vlad, down!" I called, but Seth shook his head.

"It's all right, Mom. It's... fine."

"What's up? Why on earth are you here at eight thirty in the morning? On a weekend? I know eight thirty is early for *me*, but it's downright vulgar for you!"

He didn't laugh. He didn't smile. He looked positively distraught.

"It's... Charlotte. It's... it's... happened again."

"What? What has happened again?"

I had no idea what he was talking about, but that didn't lessen my growing sense of unease. Something was terribly wrong.

"I... I tried to call, but I just got your voice mail."

I looked past him to the coffee table, where my phone sat innocently, well out of hearing because I had been in my bedroom with the door closed.

"Did you leave a message then? Why... why..." I didn't even know what I was asking him, since I had no idea why he was here.

"I did leave a message. A frantic, screaming message! And then I came here. Well, not right away. I couldn't get away right away."

He was making no sense, but he was visibly upset. I crossed

around the back of the couch and joined him, which completely flustered poor Vlad. He could sense the emotions welling up in both me and Seth, but had no outlet for his little dog response. So he just wiggled around between our two laps, trying to figure out if we needed doggy kisses or not. When in doubt, though, he'd always opt to give them. Just in case.

"Vlad... down!" Seth said, irritated and not comforted at all by the varying amounts of dog saliva hitting both sides of his face.

I picked up Vlad myself and firmly placed him back onto the floor with a firm "No!" He heeled obediently, for a change, and whimpered, flattening himself to the floor and trying to look pathetic. He succeeded, as usual.

"Okay, Seth. Tell me what happened."

"It's Charlotte."

"I knew that already. You already said that. What about Charlotte? What happened again?"

"She's... d-d-dead."

"What?"

Of course this was a superfluous thing to ask. I'd heard him just fine the first time. I just needed time to process it. A part of my mind instinctively assumed he was joking. But a larger part knew he wasn't. Not about something like this. And not just because he'd never get up before nine o'clock for a prank.

"How? Are you sure?"

"I just got done with the police at her house, so yeah. I'm pretty sure."

"I... what happened? You were at her house? Just now?"

"Yes."

"This early? On a weekend?"

"Yeah, it was the only time she said she could get together with me to get this website stuffed figured out. She wanted to take care of it as soon as possible. And... and I agreed with her, so we decided... on... this morning."

I slid closer to him on the couch and threw an arm around him. He leaned in, head on my shoulder, and closed his eyes.

"Seth, I'm so sorry."

I had to be a pillar for Seth, until I heard more about what had happened, but I was busy processing the terrible information that my friend Charlotte was dead. I had just seen her the other day, had just spoken with her on the phone yesterday. I needed to know more.

"Seth, you didn't... um..."

"Didn't what?" he asked, avoiding my gaze and scritching Vlad behind the ears instead.

"Didn't... *find* her? You know, like you found Allen?"

Seth had been the one to hold onto Allen's hand as he breathed his last there on the baseball field last year, and had even subsequently spent a night in jail when he was mistakenly thought to be the one who poisoned Allen. Something similar happening to him again this year would be nothing short of devastating.

"No, not exactly."

I exhaled the breath I didn't realize I had been holding.

"Good. I mean, not good that this happened, but good that you weren't so directly involved. But you've got to tell me more. She was fine yesterday. You said the police were there?"

"Yeah, I was supposed to meet her around seven thirty, which is crazy early for me, as you know."

"And for me. Go on."

"I get there about seven forty—I was running late—and there are cop cars with their lights flashing all around her house, in her driveway, everywhere. I wasn't even sure whether I should get out of my car or just keep driving, but I had to find out why they were there. If only to come tell you."

I patted his forearm and sighed. "Thanks. I bet that was tough for you to do. I appreciate it." My mind was racing.

"As soon as I got out of the car, a bunch of the cops were on me, not wanting me to come any closer to the front of the house. I barely got onto the grass in her front yard before they had me stop."

"Oh dear, that's not good."

"You're telling me. Anyway, they asked me why I was there, and

I told 'em I was there to help Charlotte with her website because it had been hacked."

I lifted an eyebrow at that. "I bet they found that... interesting."

"You have no idea. Anyway, I asked them what had happened, and I asked whether Charlotte was all right, because she was expecting me and I was already late."

I bit my lip and let him continue. I could see where this was going, of course, but I needed the specifics anyway.

"They told me she wouldn't be able to make whatever meeting we were supposed to have, and at that point I was still thinking that maybe she was sick or had had some sort of accident, but I didn't see an ambulance. Just a couple of cop cars... and a hearse from the coroner."

I closed my eyes and held in my breath again. This situation wasn't good for my respiration.

"They started wheeling this gurney out the front door and down the walkway, just maybe fifty feet away from me, toward the coroner's hearse."

"Oh no, it wasn't..."

"Yeah, it definitely was. Her body was covered, but since Charlotte told me that her husband and son were off on a Boy Scout camping trip for the whole weekend, I knew it had to be Charlotte under there."

I tightened my grip on his forearm and let the breath out. Along with it came the tears. For Seth, sure, but mostly for Charlotte. Whatever had happened to her, she didn't deserve it. She and Scott had a nine-year-old son, and they both doted on him. What was going to happen to Scott and Teddy now? She was young and healthy, as far as I could see. Whatever had happened to her hadn't been expected, to say the least.

"Oh, sweetie." I sighed, and he leaned onto my shoulder completely, sighing himself. I couldn't hold back a sob, and he threw his arms around me and cried.

In that moment I felt that there was nothing quite as sad or poignant as a twenty-six-year-old man crying in his mother's arms, all over something neither one of them could have changed or prevented.

Chapter 5

I T TOOK TWO DAYS FOR SCOTT to finally return the call I'd made to their landline phone. I assumed he had been deluged with other, more important phone calls from family and friends. My call, admittedly, was more from a sense of curiosity, of needing to know what had happened to my friend. But when your friend is also a fairly famous writer who was still living in her hometown and had a bazillion loyal fans, you might have to wait in line a little bit before her beleaguered, grief-stricken husband got back to you. And so I waited patiently for Scott to call. When the call came, two days after Seth had shown up at my door, I dropped everything to listen to what Scott had to say.

"It's all still a bit of a blur, Maggie," he said after I asked the obvious question about what happened. "I get this call from the police. Teddy and I are at the campground and everything. So... so..." He stopped, breathed in deeply, and let it out in a very audible sigh.

"It's all right, Scott. I don't need to hear everything."

I refrained from saying that I just needed to hear the gory parts, but that's what it felt like I was saying in the undercurrent of the conversation. I was a bad person for even thinking it.

"No, I don't mind, really. It's better than talking to the police again. I had to find a way to tell Teddy why we had to pack up everything all of a sudden and go back home. I had to decide whether to... whether to tell him right then what had happened to his mother, or try to drive all the way back home without letting on."

"Oh, Scott."

"I know. Impossible decision."

"What did you decide?"

"I told him before we even got into the car, before we even packed stuff up. It seemed better that way. Only now..."

"What?"

"Now I'm not so sure if it was better for Teddy, or just for me. So I could have someone to share it with on the drive back home."

"Scott, there's nothing wrong with sharing your grief, especially not with your son. *Charlotte's* son."

I wasn't sure I completely believed that myself, but it did no good to voice a contrary opinion to Scott right now. The poor man was suffering and had made the best choice he could at the time.

"How did Teddy take it?"

"About as bad as you'd expect. It was the worst ninety minutes of my life, that drive back home."

"I can't imagine."

"One of the other scout masters offered to pack up our gear for us and bring it back separately, so all we had to do was grab our backpacks and head out. That... that helped a lot."

"Oh, good."

"I had to force myself to drive safely. Part of me wanted to drive a hundred miles an hour to get back here. Another part of me wanted to just run the car off the road and end it all for both of us."

"Oh, Scott, no!"

"Well, it was a small part." He let out an uncomfortable laugh. "The biggest part was to just get back here safely, and that's the part that won out. Thank God."

"Yes, thank God."

"So, what happened? When you got back, I mean?"

"We had to go to the police station first, and when they were finished with us, I had to go to the morgue. But I didn't want to take Teddy with me for that, so I called my brother to come get Teddy."

"Oh, good." I was feeling rather stupid for all the generic things I was saying in response to Scott's telling me what had happened, but I honestly didn't know what else to say.

"I tell you, Maggie, going to that morgue was the hardest thing I have ever done. And I don't want to go through anything like that ever again." His breathing hitched a little bit and I could hear him holding back a full-on sob.

"Of course not. Unfortunately, Seth and I both have had to deal with similar situations in recent years. It's ugly. And horrifying. And I wish I could say that it's easy to forget, but I don't think you ever forget it."

"It changes a person."

"Yes, it does. I'm so, so sorry, Scott. Charlotte was such a good writer, and such a good friend."

"I know, Maggie. And she really appreciated you, as her proofreader and of course as her friend. You're part of the reason she made it as far as she did."

"No, her talent did that. I just tidied things up a bit for her along the way."

"Doesn't matter. She loved you for doing it. She knew you weren't always... comfortable with it."

"That was my issue, not hers. I told her that many times."

"Still. Thanks for being that sort of friend. A friend who also helped."

"I wish I could have helped more... here, at the end."

I was hoping this would lead to a smooth segue into Scott finally telling me what had happened to Charlotte. It wasn't even the stuff of local rumors yet. Scott would be my only chance at hearing what had happened anytime soon.

"Nobody could have seen this coming."

"Seen what, Scott?" I felt only slightly guilty asking outright.

"She was shot."

"Shot? As in..."

"As in... with a gun. With a bullet. Murdered."

Another sob gushed out of him, and he didn't even attempt to disguise it this time. I, on the other hand, didn't feel like sobbing. I was too stunned to sob just yet. Murdered!

"I wonder if this h-has anything to do with whoever hacked into her website."

I heard him sniffle. "Oh, yes, of course you would know about that, too. I didn't make the connection between you and Seth."

"You've spoken to Seth?" This surprised me because I was reasonably sure Seth would have mentioned it to me by now.

"No, not directly. But the police told me what he told them that morning. That... that he had come over to help her figure out what was wrong with her website. Apparently they asked him about that, and he whipped out his phone and showed them her website, with that awful skull-and-crossbones stuff all over it."

"I didn't even think to check that again. Is it still there?" Even as I was asking Scott this, I cradled the phone to my ear with my shoulder and used the mouse to bring my computer out of hibernation. I clicked the bookmark to Charlotte's website and there were the skulls and crossbones staring at me, just as they had only a few short days ago when Charlotte first called me about them.

"Yeah, still there, Maggie," Scott said, now rather unnecessarily. "Seth was coming to try to help her get rid of that stuff. Obviously that never happened. I wish it wasn't there at all."

"Maybe Seth can help get that stuff off of there. But he'll need Charlotte's password to get in and fix things."

"I know. I've been meaning to call him, to see if he can come over and sit here at Charlotte's computer. I don't know the password and wouldn't have a clue where she might have kept it written down. She probably used something obvious, but she also probably never wrote it down. So, I figured if he sat here at the same computer she used, the cookies might allow him to get into the site from here."

"That was their thinking, too. That's why he was going over there on Saturday morning."

This unsettling situation was disturbingly intriguing, and it was keeping me from thinking too much about the grief still at the bottom of my heart. At least for right now. I hadn't made the connection between the hackers and what had happened to Charlotte until now. But it made so much sense, after all. There it was right on the screen: "SOMEONE WILL DIE!" animated and writhing across the computer screen.

Just after I hung up with Scott, leaving him with too little comfort and leaving me feeling guilty about it, it occurred to me that Charlotte had disabled the website that day with me on the phone. So, why and how was it back up and running? I had a sinking feeling things were going to get worse before they got better. If they ever got better.

Chapter 6

THE NEXT MORNING I GOT A CALL from Seth, this time at an hour when I was already up and awake, so I answered it right away.

"Mom, I need a favor."

"Anything, Seth. You know that. What can I do for you'?"

"I need you to come with me over to Charlotte's house."

"What? Why?"

"Her husband wants the site taken down because it still has all that horrible stuff on it, and since neither of us knows the password Charlotte used, the only way we can think of to get it offline easily is for me to go over there and sit at her desk."

"Why can't Scott do that?"

"I... I don't know. I didn't ask."

"Heck, if I could walk Charlotte through how to disable it, you could walk Scott through it."

"Maybe at some normal point in his life, that's true. But he's still wrapped up in the funeral and, you know, missing Charlotte."

"Yes, of course. Grief. I hadn't factored that in. So, this way, it's something you can do for him, so that he doesn't have to worry about it himself."

"Precisely."

"Good then. That site needs to come down as soon as possible. It's offensive and, frankly, scary."

"I agree."

"Do the police know about it? What do they think about taking it down?"

"They want me to pay attention to anything I can find when I get into her computer, but honestly, I don't think I'll find anything they can use. My guess is that someone guessed her password and got in, or just hacked their way in from somewhere else and changed a few things."

"Guessed her password? Really? You think so?"

"Sure. I have a feeling she used something obvious as a password. Like, her son's birthday or something. Something a sick, twisted fan could guess with a little bit of digging into her personal life."

"Has Scott thought to try passwords like that himself?"

"Mom, I told you. He doesn't want to have to think about any of this. Not right now."

"Yes, yes, of course. My mistake."

"Then you'll come with me?"

"Wait, why would I need to come with you? You've met Scott before, and Teddy too."

"I know. It's just a little... you know..."

"No, Seth, I don't know. I don't mind tagging along, but I'd still like a clue about why."

I could smell the coffee brewing in the kitchen. I'd had just enough time to press the On button on the coffee maker but hadn't had time to get myself a cup before the phone rang. I contemplated putting him on speaker and getting a cup while he talked.

"Mom, you remember what happened last year. With A-Allen."

"Yeah, of course I do."

"Then let's just call this a little bit of PTSD for me. Last year you kept telling me that nobody my age should have to deal with being so closely involved in a friend's death. And now here we are a year later and it's happening all over again."

"Oh geez, of course. I didn't really make that connection for you. I was feeling a little sorry for *myself*, but I hadn't extrapolated out to *you*. I'm so sorry, sweetie."

He sighed. "It's all right. Anyway, that's why I thought of asking you to come along. I think it'll just keep me calm to have a friendly face with me."

"Is Scott not friendly?"

"No, he's fine. I just don't know him all that well. I've met Charlotte a few times, but I only met Scott once and that was mostly by accident because he came home while I was showing Charlotte how to write a new blog post on her own when I first set up her account. I'm pretty sure I'll be fine, but I wouldn't mind a little emotional backup support in case I start to feel like I'm going to have a meltdown or something. Allen's death is still too real for me."

I felt horrible that I hadn't made this connection for Seth because I'd been wrapped up in my own little world of emotions over Charlotte's death. Going with him was the least I could do.

"Should I pick you up or should we meet there separately?"

"Pick me up. Oh, thanks, Mom. I owe you one."

"No, you don't, Seth. That's what moms are for. I'll be there soon."

SCOTT WAS A GRACIOUS HOST, considering he had just lost his wife to a murderer in the same home where we were now sitting. We didn't ask him exactly where she had been found—frankly, I don't think either Seth or I even really wanted to know—but I admit I found myself glancing around the office where she wrote most of her books, looking for some sort of evidence of what had happened. At some point I realized just how creepy and vile it was to even have those thoughts, and I forced myself to get back to thinking about why we were there. Or, more precisely, why Seth was there.

"This won't take long," he said to Scott, who was barely paying attention to the details before him.

"That's fine. Whatever it takes. As long as other people can't see the website when you're done, I'll be happy."

"No problem."

"Well, not exactly *happy*," he corrected, sighing and turning away from us. "You know what I mean."

"Yes, we know," I assured him, smiling wanly and trying to seem understanding without being ingratiating or smarmy. I wasn't sure he noticed, either way. Probably just as well.

"Do you mind if I go see what Teddy is up to? I hate leaving him alone for very long. His mind starts wandering and then he kind of panics and screams for me."

He gestured toward the door that led back out into the living room, where he had left Teddy watching something innocuous on the television.

"Of course, of course! Go do what you need to do. Seth won't need any help here, or much time, from what I understand."

"Thanks, Maggie" said Scott, and he was out the door in a split second. I turned to Seth.

"How is it going? Are you in?"

"Yeah, she had cookies turned on so I just had to hit the bookmark and it got me right in. I'm just going to set it to Private for now, instead of Public. That way all the data will stay here, in case the police decide they need it later. But it won't be visible on the internet and that's the main thing right now."

"Can you see where or how those skulls and bones got onto the page in the first place? Is it there in the dashboard?"

"Looks like it's some sort of plug-in or widget that someone installed. Not harmful in and of itself. Not a virus or anything like that. Just mean-spirited and nasty."

"Well, except for the fact that she was shot three days ago, Seth. That makes it a lot worse, a lot more... nasty."

"I know that. I was speaking purely from a web geek, coding standpoint. It's not going to steal anyone's identity or anything."

"Except it kind of stole Charlotte's identity, if you know what I mean."

"Mom, are you trying to get me to have a meltdown? Because reminding me of what happened here isn't exactly helping me in the way I had hoped when I asked you to come here with me."

"Sorry. Carry on." I waved my hand vaguely toward the computer and grimaced.

"I'm done. It only took two clicks to set the site to Private. Just saved the changes. I just want to double-check by opening up another browser window and seeing if her site is still visible."

He turned away from me and back to the computer screen, opening up a second tab and clicking on the bookmark for her site.

The site came up as before, with the skull and crossbones still dancing maniacally across the screen.

"Oh no!" I exclaimed.

"Don't worry, Mom. That's a cached version of the site. If I just hit Refresh..." He clicked the mouse on the Refresh button at the top of the tabbed window and the screen redrew itself, without the skull and crossbones. And without any trace of Charlotte's blog or website. Just some placeholder text that seemed rather innocuous.

"Good!" I amended. "Much better!"

"I could have uninstalled the plug-in or widget, or whatever, but I'm still not sure the police won't want to see what's up there at some point. It would take smarter eyes than mine to dig deep enough to figure out how the widget got there in the first place, but let that be at least possible. For now, Charlotte's website is offline and no longer going to creep out any of her fans or readers who come here looking for information on her, or her death."

"Is this going to make more trouble and start more rumors, though? The site being completely gone, I mean?"

"Maybe. Do you know if she had a Facebook page, or a Twitter account?"

I nodded. "Yeah, both. She didn't use them all that much—not as much as some writers—but she had them and had a ton of followers on both. Sometimes I proofed posts before she sent them. Why?"

"Maybe those are better spots to get the word out and to dispel any rumors about what happened."

"Good thinking. I guess those are pages to visit from her computer while you're here too, right?"

"Can you go ask Scott if that's all right? Or actually, maybe we should just suggest to him that he add something personal, from him directly as her husband, when he feels up to it. I think if we let him know that it might stave off some of the inquiries he's likely to get otherwise, then he might find time to do it sooner rather than later. Kind of in his own best interests if he wants to be left alone a little more in the next few days, or weeks."

Seth was spinning around in the desk chair absently, a nervous habit I remembered from his teen years when he'd sit in my office and twirl around on my chair until he felt like puking.

"Okay, I'll go talk to him. You finish up here, and then we can get out of here. I don't like being here. And I hate that I'm saying that."

"Totally cool, Mom. I don't like being here, either. It's got me a little creeped out."

I stood and patted Seth on the shoulder as I passed him on the way out of the room. "I'll be right back to collect you and head out of here."

And so I did. Scott was fine with updating Charlotte's Facebook and Twitter pages with basic information confirming that Charlotte had indeed passed away, though whether he would eventually spill the beans about it having been a murder was another story. It was, after all, an ongoing investigation and the last thing he should do is speculate about it on the internet. Let the rumors fly. They would, and there would be no stopping them. But contribute to them directly? No, he'd already decided not to go that far for now. Wise move, I thought, and said so.

And with that settled, I collected my son and we skedaddled out of Charlotte's home and toward my own. I had a feeling my son was in desperate need of a delicious home-cooked meal. Instead, he was going to get *my* cooking. Close enough for government work.

Chapter 7

THE ENSUING DAYS AND WEEKS led to a lot of speculation about what had happened to Charlotte. Because it was a murder investigation, it found its way into the local paper. And once it was in the local paper, it traveled easily and quickly to other parts of the country. God bless the internet, right?

For the most part I could avoid the topic of Charlotte if I wanted to. I wasn't a big Facebook junkie to begin with, and if I avoided any hashtags on Twitter that involved Charlotte or her books, I could dodge that topic completely. What made it tough were the emails and even the phone calls. Her agent called me—to commiserate since we'd both maintained dual professional and personal relationships with Charlotte over the years—and I wasn't really of a mind to commiserate. I was strictly a conflict-avoidance person and always had been. And things like a friend's murder fell squarely into the conflict category.

I was sick of talking about this. I was sick of thinking about this. I couldn't imagine how Scott was getting through it, since he was faced with huge changes to his personal life, huge amounts of loss, plus juggling the emotions and problems of his now-motherless son, Teddy.

The police didn't contact us again—me or Seth—which was a huge relief to us both. Seth spent that first week wound tight as a spring over worrying that he was going to have to testify or give a statement or something else equally horrifying or reminiscent of his experiences of last year with Allen's death. After the second week of relative quiet from the police, he began to unravel a little bit and relax. When a third week passed, he began to wonder just what the police were thinking because, the more *he* thought about it, the more he was sure that there was a connection between the skulls and crossbones and whoever had killed Charlotte. I had to agree. Between that website hack and the entire genre in which she wrote, I was sure there were connections all over the place that the police were apparently not making. I started to think it might be time to lend the police a hand and point them in the right direction. Just a little bit.

But of course, the police didn't want my help. They didn't ask for my help. I hadn't expected them to. I wanted to get to the bottom of this, sooner rather than later, but I also wanted nothing more to do with it. That was a dilemma, for sure. I couldn't have it both ways.

In the meantime, Scott had started posting updates to Charlotte's Facebook page, and he sent out a tweet saying he was her husband and that her Twitter account would remain open. The response was fairly positive, with only the occasional complaint from a disgruntled fan who wanted more access to Charlotte's private life—and death. I occasionally checked in on her Facebook page and took a peek at her Twitter feed, and I wasn't learning a whole lot about what might be going on with the investigation. Should I find a way to weasel my way into their good graces or just keep flying below the radar and leave well enough alone?

I ARRIVED AT THE COFFEE SHOP about a half hour early, hoping to get a little bit of work done on the laptop before Scott and Seth arrived. Scott had asked to meet both of us, without giving us much clue what he wanted. We had both agreed, if only to help out a newly widowed young father.

A small corner table by the window looked cozy enough, so I set down my tray with the lunch kolache on it and then went up front to fill my coffee cup. It felt soothing and right to be here again after too much time away. I'd often met clients here to discuss their projects or otherwise just to share a coffee once a book finally came out in print, and the last time I had been here was to catch up with Charlotte herself when I'd finished proofing her last book.

Although the plate glass window felt cold to the touch because of the lower temperatures outside, the sun streaming in from the clear blue sky above warmed me as I sat waiting for my son and Scott. I wrapped my hands around the coffee cup, which was almost too hot—almost—and sighed. What could Scott possibly want that he had to meet with both me and Seth like this? He had sounded cryptic and elusive on the phone yesterday, and I had agreed despite a few misgivings about the strange urgency in his voice. At least Seth would be here with me too, in case Scott was coming a bit unhinged and needed a little grounding from some friends. Sure, we weren't *great* friends—I knew Charlotte a lot better than I knew him, and I'd only met him a few times when I'd been at their house, usually at the beginning or the end of one of Charlotte's book projects. But right now we were artificially close, the three of us brought together by Charlotte's death. Plus, I think Scott appreciated that we had some heartfelt emotions about Charlotte and yet had just enough professional restraint because our relationships with his wife had originated through work-related tasks.

I'd always had a tendency to develop friendships with my proofreading clients, especially if I had a chance to meet with them in person. So, my friendship with Charlotte these past few years was nothing weird or out of the ordinary. But I now felt I was in a bit of a freefall, emotionally speaking. Two years ago I'd had the unfortunate experience of stumbling upon the murdered body of the town's new newspaper editor in his office when I was headed in there to meet with him about proofreading the newspaper, a job

I had done for years with the prior editor. And yet, there he lay, Lee Gerber, sprawled across his desk with a bloody letter opener sticking up out of his back. Nasty luck that, because the overly long, overly sharp letter opener had punctured his heart. Nasty luck for me, too, because to this day I couldn't completely rid myself of that image or the pain and anguish of the weeks that followed. And Lee Gerber hadn't even been a friend. I had only met him a short time before, and he'd never struck me as someone I could ever call a friend anyway.

Then, last year, Seth and I had watched one of his baseball teammates die from poisoning—another murder. Seth still occasionally had nightmares about it, so I hoped to minimize his involvement in this current situation. It was becoming a bit of a habit, one of us tripping over a dead body or encountering a situation in which we became embroiled in yet another local murder. If I wasn't careful I was going to get a reputation like that Jessica What's Her Name woman on television. Only I wasn't going to get paid umpteen thousand dollars per episode. At least I didn't think so. That probably would have only covered the ensuing therapy sessions anyway.

So, now, to have to go through something similar for a third time in as many years felt a tad ridiculous. Did anybody but private investigators and detectives on television shows have this much bad luck with murder victims? Was I some sort of killing victim magnet or something?

As I continued to muse along these lines, gripping the coffee cup a little harder with each passing thought, to the point where I was dangerously close to crushing it and sending hot coffee all over my lap, I heard a low, male cough to my right. Looking up, I saw Seth standing next to the table I had claimed, clutching his own coffee cup and smiling broadly.

"Seth!"

"Hi! You're early."

"Yeah, I wanted to see if I could get a little work done first."

He looked at the table, which did not have my laptop on it yet, just the now-empty tray and plate, with a few stray kolache crumbs giving away what I had actually been doing for the past half hour.

"How's that working out for you then?" His smile widened into a crazy grin and I smacked his knee and pointed to the chair across from mine.

"Sit, and behave, would you? Scott's due here soon, so let's maintain a suitable sense of gravity when he's here."

"Do we even know why he wants us here? Has he told you anything since I talked to you last night?"

I shook my head. "Nope. Just that it was important and it involved a favor from both of us."

He pulled out the chair with his free hand and plopped down hard, as if he had just run a marathon.

"You all right?"

"Yeah..."

He didn't sound all right.

"Well, *that* sounded convincing. Not." I smiled. And, better yet, he smiled back. I instantly felt better. He was hanging in there.

"It's fine. I just wish I knew what Scott was up to asking us here. Makes me a little nervous."

"Me too," I admitted.

"You don't suppose something has happened, do you? You know, with the police?"

"No, we would have heard something about that."

We had no time to muse about Scott's motives because I looked up to see him coming in the front door of the café.

"Looks like we're about to find out what's up with Scott," said Seth after he followed my line of sight and saw Scott, too.

I flagged Scott down and he headed in our direction instead of going to the front counter to order something. He pulled up the third chair at the little table and sat immediately.

"Didn't mean to sidetrack you," I said. "Get something to eat or a cup of coffee or something."

"In a minute. I wanted to give you these as soon as I could, Maggie." He swung a messenger bag off his shoulder and flipped open the canvas flap on its front. I glanced at Seth and raised an eyebrow in question. He simply shrugged and looked back at Scott, who was now pulling out two large binder-clipped bunches of paper. I'd been around writers long enough to recognize manuscripts when I saw them.

"Manuscripts," I said, stating the obvious.

"Yes, ma'am," said Scott and unceremoniously dumped the stack onto the table, missing the tray of kolache crumbs by a small margin. "I found these in the deep file drawer of Charlotte's desk yesterday."

"What are they?" I asked as I turned the stack toward me and casually leafed through the pages of the top manuscript.

"Novels, I think."

"Novels, as in *unpublished* novels?"

"Yup. Two of them."

The stacks were hefty, double-spaced, regular margins. "These look like *complete* novels, too."

"As far as I can tell, yes. Both of them."

"Any reason she would have printed out complete novel manuscripts and just put them in a desk drawer?" I was still flipping through the pages.

"No idea. There wasn't anything else in that drawer, no notes, no nothing. I don't know if this is how she usually worked or not. That's why I had to see you. Do you know if she'd print out certain drafts of works in progress? Maybe to scribble on them? Or to give them to you, maybe? To proofread? Maybe she was just ahead of schedule and had a backlog of finished stories?"

"No, Scott, as far as I know, she didn't routinely print out rough drafts on paper. Or, frankly, finished drafts, either. She and I worked through the word processor's Track Changes feature. I used to work from hard copy for years—and I still have an editing desk my dad made me—but I haven't done work on paper for a novelist for a long time. And, never for Charlotte."

"I hate to ask this then, but was she... happy?"

"Happy about what?" I must have had quite the blank look on my face because I had no clue what he could be getting at.

"About... gee, I hate to even ask this, but I'm exploring all options now that I've found these things."

"Go on, then. You won't hurt my feelings."

I realized I couldn't guarantee that as soon as I said it. I had pretty thick skin as far as my work was concerned, but who knew what he was going to ask me next?

"Was she happy, Maggie? With your work? Your proofreading?"

"As far as I know, Scott. What would that have to do with... oh, I see where you're going with this. You think she might have printed these out to give to a different proofreader? Someone who maybe works with hard copy?"

He nodded, looking uncomfortable at the implications of his question.

"No, I seriously doubt it. For one thing, the next stage after an early draft might be an editor, but not a proofreader."

"What's the difference?"

It was a common mistake. Editing and proofreading often got mixed up in people's minds.

"Well, her editor would be a developmental editor, someone who would walk her through any plot holes or character development issues. Things like that. Problems with the story itself. Some editors will also point out issues a proofreader would catch, but that's not their main focus."

"Can you tell from looking at these if they've been through a developmental editor yet?"

I continued to turn pages on the top manuscript. "Not really, no. Not without reading it completely. And even then, Charlotte had a bunch of novels already under her belt. Meaning that perhaps these are rough drafts but aren't *too* rough because she's a seasoned writer. Or, *was* a seasoned writer."

I blushed at my mistake, but Scott didn't seem to notice it.

"How can I tell? If you read these, Maggie, would you be able to tell if they were ready to go to a proofreader?"

"Probably not. Have you thought to ask her editor? Perhaps he's seen these manuscripts and has asked her to fix some things."

"But why would she have printed them out?"

"A lot of writers will edit their own work with printouts at some stage. Lots of folks says it's a good way to catch mistakes and problems that get missed on the computer screen. Changing up the medium from screen to paper changes how you see the words on the page. On the literal page, in this case. Does that make sense?"

"Yah, a ton of sense. No, I didn't ask her editor yet. I don't know that guy. He's in New York, I think. But since I know you and Seth, and since you're both right here and are kinda involved in all this mess already, I figured I'd start by asking you what you think is going on with these."

"I wish I could help you more, Scott. Have you looked on her computer for these titles? There have to be documents or something on the computer with these things. Maybe your clues are there. She might have a folder for each of these projects, with other things in the folders, like files with ideas or notes or plans, or something."

"Already checked. No trace of files with these titles on them. Unless she started them with different titles and just never changed the names of the files."

"Have you gone through her emails to her editor? You know, to find out if they've been corresponding about these projects? I just can't see Charlotte—or any writer—writing two complete novels, printing them out, and then stuffing them in a desk drawer without any word to anyone about them. She didn't mention to me anything about other book projects. As far as I knew, that last book we worked on together was her most recent work. And, the only work still not published."

"You mean, the one the publisher now wants to put out posthumously?"

"Seriously?" I sighed. "Well, of course they do. They already have a contract for it, and they have it complete and in hand already. So of course they're going to publish it." I was half talking to myself at this point, but Scott heard me.

"Yeah, I knew I had no choice but to let them go ahead with it."

"Would you have said no if you had the chance?"

"I don't know," he said, gesturing and running his hand through his hair. "But I think I would have appreciated the choice."

"Business is business, though."

"Apparently."

Just then Seth coughed from his spot in between me and Scott.

"Oh, hi, Seth! Didn't mean to ignore you there." Scott smiled at Seth, who smiled as cheerily as he could. He hated uncomfortable moments of silence or lulls in a conversation. Plus, I had a strange feeling he was still wondering why Scott had asked him here.

"Hi, Scott. Sorry you're still going through all this."

"Mmph." Scott lowered his eyes and hid the rest of his face for a moment.

"What help can I give you in all this?"

"Oh, yes. Sorry," Scott said, looking up and sitting straighter in his chair. "I didn't mean to let you sit there unnoticed."

"No problem. Seriously. You can only talk to one of us at a time, after all. Right?"

There was that smile again. It looked almost painted on. I would have to talk to Seth about his people skills later. He had moments where he seemed almost creepy. I knew he was a computer geek and therefore prone to a dearth of social skills, but the fake smile had to go. Scott was too preoccupied with his own underlying situation to have noticed, though. Perhaps I noticed it because I was Seth's mother and therefore still prone to finding fault where I shouldn't. Either way, a short pep talk was in order.

"And now it's time to talk to you," Scott said, facing Seth directly. "I'm wondering why the police don't seem overly concerned about the hacker situation that happened on Charlotte's site."

"I am too," agreed Seth.

"So, this sort of thing isn't completely run of the mill then? Doesn't happen all the time?"

"I'd say no, though it's of course not completely rare, either. It's definitely something the police should be taking seriously."

"And I don't think they are."

Seth frowned and hunched forward in the chair. "That's

disturbing. Unless they have more solid leads somewhere else right now."

"Not that they've told me, no. But then again, I have no idea how much they're obligated to tell me. Even if I am Charlotte's husband."

"Maybe it's because you *are* Charlotte's husband," I added.

"Meaning what?" asked Scott, now frowning himself.

"Meaning, isn't it typical to look first at the spouse in cases of murder like this? Or other close family members?"

His frown turned into a look of alarm and he sat back. "Seriously?"

"Seriously."

"I guess I would have thought that was the stuff of books and movies."

"It is. For a reason."

"Well, what am I supposed to do about that, Maggie?"

"Keep doing what you're doing. Nothing more. But nothing less."

I was relatively certain that Scott didn't have anything to do with Charlotte's murder. Theirs wasn't a cheesy, gushy-romantic relationship, but it was solid and based on all the right things, from what I could see. Their had son seemed well adjusted and happy. And Charlotte had the life she wanted, with a husband who supported her dreams. It was a lot more than a lot of us could ask for.

The situation just didn't seem like one mirroring those of books and movies. But I also hoped I was right in that assertion. The alternative was difficult to contemplate.

"But what if the police are acting this way and not taking me seriously because they suspect me?" His voice broke a bit on the word "suspect" and I felt so badly for him, dealing with the loss of his wife, plus the responsibility of their son, who was facing his own grief demons right now, too. To add, on top of all that, the idea—no matter how remote—that the police might actually be scrutinizing him because there was a chance he had killed her... well, it would be too much for just about anybody to bear well.

"I don't know, Scott," I said, feeling particularly unhelpful.

"I was hoping, Seth, that this is where you could help me. I've been assuming that they're ignoring my ideas because I know so little about computers. I'm strictly an end user."

"So am I," I added, trying to sound helpful, "which is why having Seth around is so helpful." I smiled.

"I thought maybe Seth could help me by coming to the police station with me and explaining why this needs to be taken seriously. I thought they'd listen to someone who does this sort of thing for a living."

I continued to smile, but as I glanced over at Seth, I could see exactly what I expected to see. He was trying to look cheerful again, and yet I could tell he felt cornered. I knew the last thing he wanted to do was get involved with the police and another murder. The last time he'd tried to help out, he'd ended up in the slammer, to coin a phrase. He'd been quickly exonerated, but the experience had left an indelible mark on his psyche. One I didn't fancy exposing him to a second time.

"Do you really need Seth?" I asked. "He's... been through this before and didn't enjoy it."

"It's okay, Mom," Seth interjected. "I'll help."

I sighed and reached across the table to grab his hand, but he flinched a little and withdrew it onto his lap.

Whatever was going to happen here, it wasn't going to be fun.

Again.

Chapter 8

I TOOK THE TWO MYSTERY MANUSCRIPTS HOME with me, trying to think of a good time to work into my freelance schedule. Once I was in the door of my apartment, I dropped the keys and purse onto the side table just inside the front door, put the manuscripts on the couch, and grabbed Vlad's leash off the hook there. He was already wiggling his furry butt all around my ankles and feet—a typical reaction to the sight of his leash in my hand.

"All right, buddy," I said, leaning down and clipping the leash onto his collar. "Let's take a quick walk today. I have a lot of work to do."

I was suddenly grateful that Vlad was really bad at telling time and had no idea what I meant by a "quick walk." He had to go badly enough that we barely made it into the backyard before he was lifting his little doggy leg on the nearest dogwood tree. As soon as his leg hit the ground again I was turning and heading back to the apartment building.

"C'mon. Git along, little doggy." Vlad trotted along behind me, unaware that we weren't going anywhere else but back inside. He hesitated a little bit at the front door to the building, but with a little coaxing (and a little tugging on that leash), he scampered into the apartment ahead of me and wiggled around in place just inside the door, waiting for me to bend down and unclip the leash from his collar. As soon as I had unhooked it, Vlad dashed away from me into the kitchen. I heard loud slurping as he gulped down water from his water dish.

"Slow down, Vlad! The last thing I want is for you to throw up all that water on my couch!"

Once Vlad was settled back into his little doggy bed under the oversized desk in my office, I sank into my comfy chair across the room and grabbed the first manuscript, pinching the oversized binder clip to take it off. I held the stack of papers firmly so that I wouldn't have to retrieve a loose pile from the floor at my feet, and I sighed with an anticipation that was part curiosity and part emotional fatigue. All three of my current clients had their projects back on their plates, and I was still waiting for any sort of response from any of them. Might as well use the downtime to see what I could glean from Charlotte's unseen manuscripts. I braced myself for just about anything in terms of content. If these were newer manuscripts, they were probably a lot edgier than her earlier work. She seemed to grow bolder with each novel, which only garnered her more readers and stronger accolades. I worried that perhaps these manuscripts had been hidden because they were a little too bold, even for Charlotte.

Of course, perhaps they were earlier manuscripts—ones she never intended to see the light of day. That wouldn't really explain why she had chosen to print them out, though. Paper wasn't exactly cheap, so printing out a double-spaced manuscript on one side of the paper added up fast. Besides, these days there were few circumstances when a writer needed to print out a manuscript— not for an editor, not for an agent. Email attachments were the way everybody worked now. I'd stowed away my folding editor's desk a few years ago and hadn't needed to drag it out any time since.

If Charlotte had printed them out for herself, that might make some sense. A lot of authors still swore by self-editing done on actual paper with a real pen. Sometimes it was easier to see one's own mistakes on paper. But, in those situations, most people would use scrap paper just to save some money. These manuscripts were printed on good, clean paper on one side only. As if they were going to be sent to someone.

But if so, why were they languishing in a desk drawer and not out on her desk or elsewhere in her office where she could package them up and send them wherever they needed to go?

Before I even started reading, there were already so many unanswered questions. I hoped my reading answered some of them for me.

Unfortunately, though, I got only a few pages into the novel before I was more confused than ever. I was somewhere near the end of chapter one when I heard myself say out loud, rather loudly, "What the *hell* is going on here?"

The story made almost no sense. The characters weren't Charlotte's usual well-drawn folks. Half of what she was writing seemed more like stream of consciousness. Sure, that was often a good technique for getting the writing flowing on a day filled with writer's block, but it certainly wasn't something someone did for three hundred pages and then printed out and tucked neatly into a drawer with a binder clip on it to keep everything tidy.

I laid the manuscript alongside me on the chair and stood up. Across the room I retrieved a spiralbound notebook I used for all sorts of scribbling and scrawling, and I grabbed a pen off the computer desk. I plopped back into my chair and hoisted the loose manuscript pages onto my lap, topping it off with the spiralbound notebook. I turned back the cover and clicked the ballpoint pen a few times. I found there were almost too many disjointed, unformed questions in my mind right now, and I had no certain, clear way to express them. So, I started doodling on the paper and hoped I'd find a way to voice my queries. After a few minutes of scribbling circles and shapes on the top of the page, I settled in to jot down thoughts regarding the first chapter of this first manuscript.

- *What is going on here? What is the reader supposed to know or learn?*
- *Why are these characters so cardboard?*
- *Why is some of the dialogue artificially stilted? Some of these characters start their sentences and responses in odd ways that don't sound natural.*
- *Why is the formatting a little bit off? Paragraphs don't seem to break where you'd think paragraphs would naturally break.*
- *Why does this NOT sound anything like Charlotte's other books?*

There were other questions in my mind, but these got me started. I sat for a while, glancing and flipping through the manuscript again, trying to see anything of Charlotte in what I was reading. Later chapters seemed even more forced than the first one, and I wouldn't have thought that possible.

I gave myself another half hour of reading this particular manuscript before deciding that this was either the worst first draft I had ever read or that something else was going on here. I was going to have to let this simmer in my brain for a while because no easy, clear answers were forthcoming. I put down the first manuscript after fastening it once again with the large binder clip and took up the second manuscript, sighing audibly in anticipation of more of the same.

Sadly, I was right in my apprehension. More strangely written, awkwardly worded prose, from a woman who was a very good writer. I had read so many of Charlotte's earlier manuscripts that I had seen a progression in her writing skills. She was good, even in the beginning, but her style had developed into a polished talent that was evident even if you didn't read her genre. So, thinking back on her earlier work, I tried to make sense of what I was reading now. Could this in fact simply be an early work with a lot less of the skill I had come to expect from Charlotte? I kept coming back to the same answer, the more I asked myself this question as I continued to read: No. This just wasn't Charlotte. And yet, the first pages of both transcripts had her name right at the top of every page in the header: Charlotte Collins. And, of course, these were found in her desk drawer, in her office, in her house. Hard to say they were forgeries written by someone else, or even bad fan fiction.

I put this second manuscript on my lap and pondered the situation. What other explanation could account for all the facts? Well, the "facts" as I currently understood them, anyway. I gave up and clipped this manuscript back together, too, setting them both on the end table next to the chair. Time to run a few errands. And maybe I would stop in and say hello to Helga at the Brighton *Bugle* while I was out. Sometimes she gave me a good laugh and helped me to gain a better perspective on a situation. Not much had been funny in the past few weeks, and although I didn't want to minimize Charlotte's death, I also knew I had to get out of this funk and get back to work. And if I was going to be any help to Scott at all, I'd have to straighten up and refocus my wee brain onto something else. All work and no play, and all that rot. Plus, I could usually talk Helga into going out for Chinese food at the drop of a hat. Time for a little comfort food distraction for me, and a little inane pointless joking from Helga.

"Sure, chickie. You know I'm always up for a little frivolity." Helga beamed at me from across the high counter in the foyer of the Brighton *Bugle's* office. Helga had been a staple at this front desk for as long as I could remember, certainly as long as I had been proofreading the newspaper as a freelancer. She'd seen a lot of other workers come and go, from reporters to ad salesmen to typesetters, and even editors. Our newest editor, Alfred Thomas, had come on board only two years earlier when the previous editor, Lee Gerber, had been murdered. Lee's tenure had been especially short lived, a blip on the radar of the paper's history. He'd come into the job with a bad history behind him—notably a disgruntled author with whom he had worked at his previous job at a small publishing house.

Were we sorry to see him go? Except for the obvious unwilling-ness to enjoy the death of a fellow human being, no, not really. He'd never quite fit in here in the small town of Brighton. The new editor was a much better fit, if you asked me. Actually, if you asked any-body. Everybody loved Alfred. Helga had always loved her job—she was about as extroverted as you could get—but having a boss she truly admired and liked made it even better. It was nice to see the paper thriving again, even if it was struggling now in the digital age. Struggling and adapting were a lot easier when you liked the people you were working with.

So, as expected, Helga was happy and gleeful when I came in, and not because I was a distraction from the dull drudgery of her work. The enthusiasm was contagious, and I smiled back at her.

"Good, because I've had a hankering for some General Tso's for ages but just haven't worked it into my schedule."

"You just didn't want to eat alone, that's all," Helga said, winking and chomping on her gum more loudly than seemed humanly possible.

"You know I *love* to eat alone, Helga. It's what I live for. You should feel grateful that I'm allowing you to share the experience with me for a change."

"You're such a... hermit, Maggie." She said it with affection but I smirked anyway.

"You say that like it's a bad thing," I countered.

She winked again. "For me, it would be. I'd be mortified to have to eat alone."

"Well, to be fair, I wouldn't sit in the *restaurant* all alone. I'd order takeout and eat it at home."

"In your jammies? Watching the Lifetime Channel?"

"No, of course not!"

She raise an eyebrow at me in question.

"Back episodes of *Ozark*. Duh." I grinned.

"That sounds like you. C'mon. Let's blow this popsicle stand."

"I have no idea what that means, but I guess it means we're leaving."

She stood and grabbed her purse from off the back of her desk chair. She sashayed around the high counter and joined me in front of it, in the lobby. "We're out of here, cutie!"

Yeah, I needed this evening out something fierce.

"So, LET ME GET THIS STRAIGHT," said Helga after I had finished catching her up on all the excitement with Scott. Well, "excitement" was perhaps a strong term in this case, but it felt a little more exciting once I was sharing it with Helga, who was always up for a good challenge of the intellect. I wouldn't say she was intellectual, really, but she could think outside the box like nobody's business. It was almost scary. I figured it couldn't hurt to have her perspective on those two odd manuscripts. A fresh pair of eyes—or ears—and all that.

"Scott, her husband, gives you these two manuscripts to read and is hoping what? That you'll proofread them so he can publish them? Or something else?"

"He didn't exactly say. But that's what I'm assuming, yes. That he thinks these are publishable and can maybe bring in some money. I can't imagine he won't be hurting without her book royalties coming in from any more new books."

"And you don't think these are all that good? Not good enough to publish? Or just not good enough to publish under her name?"

"All of the above, really. Her fans wouldn't like them. They're not up to Charlotte's standards."

"But they both have Charlotte's name on them?"

"Yup, clear as day. Right from her desk drawer. Looking like she had just printed them out the day before."

"So what's the dilemma, Maggie? Proofread them for ol' Scotty Boy and be done with it. After all, you're losing a steady client too, so you might as well get a last project out of the situation, right?"

"Only you could find the financial perspective in all this, Helga."

"Hey, money makes the world go 'round, sweets. Everybody knows that."

She poked around on her plate of lo mein with one of her chopsticks as she spoke. I'd finished nearly all of my General Tso's chicken and was working on the rest of my pork fried rice, using a respectable fork and spoon rather than the eternally frustrating chopsticks that Helga knew how to use deftly. I wasn't nearly so coordinated and never even bothered to try to use them anymore, especially in public. I just embarrassed myself every time. Although, come to think of it, they would certainly be a good diet device since I could barely get any food to my mouth with the blasted things.

"What else could be going on here, though? It's not like it's early Charlotte. These stories are both just... weird. Like they were cobbled together from several different stories without any regard for good storytelling. I could barely follow what was supposed to be going on."

"Have you seriously entertained the thought that they weren't written by Charlotte at all?" She had scooped up those slippery lo mein noodles like they were yarn on a grandmother's knitting needles. How did she do that?

"How can that be true, though?" I asked. "They have her name on them and they were in her own desk."

"Well, there are other possibilities," Helga said casually, as if the answers were dangling right in front of her like those lo mein noodles and she could just as easily scoop those up for me and hand them to me across the table.

"Like what?" I said. Apparently I had completely lost all ability to think creatively about this situation because I saw no other possibility.

"Like... Scott wrote them."

"Scott? Her husband Scott?"

"No, Scott Baio. Scott Pilgrim. Sheesh, Maggie. Yes, of course I mean her husband." She winked at me, a Helga habit that I typically found endearing, except when she had bested me in some way. Then it started to feel irksome. That was my issue, though, not hers.

"How could Scott have written those two stories, though?"

"What do you mean, how? With a computer, the same way Charlotte wrote hers. It's not that hard to understand, not really."

By now the lo mein was disappearing fast. My fried rice was also not long for this world, but it was oh, so good. I was glad I had suggested Chinese food. It was just what I needed. Now, if I could convince her to go to Hank's Scoops for some ice cream afterwards, we'd be all set. But for now, I had to get my mind around what she had just said. And for some reason, my mind didn't want to go there.

"But, *he* is the one who gave me both of those manuscripts in the first place!"

She smiled demurely, which was a tough thing for ol' Helga to do. "So, what does that tell you then, about ol' Scotty Boy?"

"That he—"

"That he what?" I felt like she was a trial attorney leading me on in a cross examination.

"That he lied to me?"

"You catch on fast, chickie." The last bit of lo mein swirled around her chopsticks and slapped into her mouth with a grace I would never have while eating Chinese food. Or, really, any food. Perhaps some of my introversion had its roots in my poor eating skills. Sometimes I thought I should buy some sort of full-body bib for adults, if they made such a thing. I'd have to check Amazon later.

"That makes absolutely no sense. Why in the world would Scott write not one, but *two* terrible stories—stories even *he* could have written better than that—then put his wife's name on them both, print them out, and put them in her desk drawer, only to take them back out and give them to me to proofread for him?"

"Well, I don't know that part yet, do I? You're the one with the amazing attention to detail, remember?"

I frowned at her and put down my fork and spoon, which clanked onto the plate a little too loudly. There wasn't anyone at the tables immediately surrounding us, though, so my rude gesture went unnoticed, even by Helga.

"That's with spelling and punctuation, Helga, not murder and mayhem."

She shook her head. "Nope. Not the way I remember it. You have definitely been developing a knack for cutting through the bullshit in situations like this. I'm surprised you didn't see this for what it clearly is."

"How can I even think it was Scott? I mean, the man loved his wife and loved her writing. Why would he suddenly want to write, and put *her* name on them? Why not just write his own bad stories?"

"Well, I don't know the man all that well—not as well as you or Seth know him—but the objective part of me standing outside of this situation says that perhaps he knows more than he is telling."

"You mean... wait, no, you don't mean..."

"Why yes, the more I think about it, the more I think I *do* mean..."

"That's absurd."

"Is it?"

"Yes!"

"Okay, if you say so." She reached for one of the fortune cookies on a small tray sitting at the far end of our booth. She calmly unwrapped the cellophane and extracted the cookie in one deft movement. I watched as she crunched the small cookie without saying another word. I could tell she was waiting for my brain to catch up to hers. It's not that I wasn't smart enough to think of something as strangely obvious as Scott being a liar (and whatever other implications came along with that). It was just that I thought I knew Scott well enough to glean whether he was lying to me—and to Seth, come to think of it. I just didn't sense that level of deception from Scott. Not about this, anyway. But I'd been wrong about things before. And I had no other hunches about these weird stories that were supposedly penned by Charlotte. Scott having written them instead would certainly explain why they didn't sound at all like Charlotte's writing. But it didn't explain why they were so obtuse and difficult to comprehend. Even a non-writer like Scott could likely come up with better storytelling than I found in either of those abominations. I hesitated to call them stories. They were that bad.

I frowned and leaned across the booth to Helga, in order to speak more quietly. Even without people in the immediate vicinity, I didn't want to risk being overheard. After all, the story of Charlotte's murder would soon become all everyone in town could talk about.

"So, let me get this straight. If you think Scott is lying to me about these stories, then what else do you think he's lying about?"

"You tell me."

"I can't tell you! I don't think he wrote them!"

"But you don't think Charlotte wrote them, either."

"Definitely not."

"Then that narrows it down. Did their son write them?"

"He's nine. Don't be ridiculous."

"Well, you said they aren't very good. Couldn't he have written them if they're bad? Like, nine-year-old-kid bad?"

"No, they're not amateurish. They're... strange. Odd. *Off*, somehow. I can't really explain it."

"I can see that," she said, with another of her winks.

I smiled. "Very funny, Helga. You do realize where your assumptions are starting to lead us, right?"

"I sure do. But I'm just ruling out other possibilities. If Charlotte didn't write these, and yet they have her name on them and were in her house, what other options do you have? I'm pretty sure you don't think that someone broke into their house and put them there, right?"

I laughed out loud. "No, not really. Although that would certainly be an easy way out of this mess right about now."

"It would probably answer a lot more questions that it would bring up, that's for sure." She winked at me yet again.

"Would you kindly stop that winking at me? It's starting to look like you have an eye twitch or something." We both laughed.

"Unsolved murders and lying husbands always make my eye twitch, Maggie."

"Then your eyes would have been twitching for years if you'd been married to George like I was."

She snorted with laughter. "Oh, sweetie, you're learning. A few more lessons in the Sarcasm of Helga Schmutt course and you'll be ready to graduate with honors." One more wink for good measure.

"All kidding aside," I added, looking serious and reaching for my own fortune cookie across the booth. "How likely do you think it is?"

"How likely do I think what is?"

"C'mon, don't act coy now. If Scott's lying and trying to foist stories on me as if they are his wife's and not his, then all bets are off, right? Meaning, he could be hiding all sorts of other facts from me. From... the police. Right? That's where this could lead."

"Well, don't the police usually assume it's the husband in a case like this?"

"Yes, yes, yes. Seth and I had this conversation with Scott the other day, in fact. It hadn't occurred to him that the police might be eyeing him as a potential suspect."

"How do you know?"

"He told us."

She just smiled at me across the table, tapping one of her chopsticks on her plate in a strangely syncopated rhythm.

"Uh huh."

"Okay okay, I see where you went with that. Very funny."

"It doesn't seem the least bit funny to me, Maggie. Not really."

"Then why are you grinning at me from across this table?"

"Because toying with you is funny, that's why."

"You're incorrigible, Helga. You truly are."

"Aw, toots. You love me. You know you do."

I nodded. "Yeah, I do. And I don't necessarily think you're wrong. It's just not an option that had occurred to me."

"Because you're too close to the situation, that's why."

"But sometimes that closeness means you know people better and can more accurately judge their possible behavior. Isn't that so?"

"Sure, sure. But your way keeps leading to a dead end, right? So I figured it was time to look at this with a different path in mind. It's certainly possible. And statistically, it's even likely. Isn't it? At least compared to the reverse-thief theory?"

I cracked open the fortune cookie and read the slip of paper inside to myself: *You will soon go on a new adventure.*

Helga saw me brooding over the fortune cookie. "What's it say, chickie?"

"I'd rather not say."

"Aw, c'mon. Humor an old lady for once."

I tossed the little slip of paper across the table at her, where it landed squarely in the middle of her empty plate. She scooped it up and read it, then burst into laughter. "Oh, that's rich!" she said, snorting with laughter and dropping the fortune back onto her plate. "Can I go on this big adventure with you?"

"Don't you always?" I replied, and we both grinned at each other.

"I certainly do."

I popped the crunchy cookie into my mouth and bit down on it. Helga just smiled.

"Let's get the check and get outta here, shall we?"

"Not a moment too soon."

Chapter 9

HAD ENJOYED BEING OUT WITH HELGA, but of course the direction our conversation had gone toyed with my emotions the rest of the evening once I was back home. Vlad sensed the tension immediately and kept trying to curl up alongside me on the couch as I flipped through the television channels angrily. I wasn't finding the sort of distraction I needed right now, and Vlad's incessant wiggling at my side had segued beyond helpful and well into annoying. It wasn't his fault, of course, so I tried not to be harsh with him. But I was quite ready to call it a night and head off to bed, where I could close the bedroom door and leave poor Vlad out here in the apartment to fend for himself for the rest of the night. Maybe I would find better distraction in a good book instead of the television, which seemed suddenly filled with nothing more than cop shows and police procedurals. Great. Not exactly the stuff of distraction from my present thoughts about Scott.

And just what *were* my present thoughts about Scott? Even I wasn't sure anymore. He had seemed so incredibly sincere in his conversation with me and Seth, and he certainly seemed stunned to learn that he might be on the short list as a suspect in his own wife's murder. I was sure I wasn't wrong in my interpretation of those events. Maybe in the morning I'd call Seth and see if his impression was any different from mine. I could tell him about the manuscripts first and ask if his conclusions were anything like Helga's. He had been there with me, so his opinion meant more to me than Helga's. It was important to get this murder solved—the whole town was abuzz with talk of it, and not in a good way—but it was also important not to jump to conclusions and get poor Scott in trouble if his actions and motives didn't warrant it. I couldn't be that bad a judge of character, could I?

"No, I don't believe that for a minute," said Seth after I had laid out everything for him that Helga and I had gone over the evening before. "You don't believe it, do you, Mom?"

"No, I don't. Or, at least, I don't want to. But now that I've got these two novel manuscripts here, I'm not sure what to do about this new information. It's... vexing."

"Vexing? Who uses a word like '*vexing*'?"

"Apparently I do. Now, can we go on with this, please?"

He chuckled under his breath, which I could sense even over the bad phone connection.

"Ever since dinner with Helga last night, I've been racking my brain trying to come up with a better explanation than hers. So far, I can't think of anything. I was hoping you could help me. I don't want to go down the road of Scott being involved in Charlotte's murder."

"No, neither do I. It doesn't seem possible. I know I don't know Scott all that well, but it... doesn't seem possible."

"So you said, yes."

"So you're back to Charlotte having written them then? The stories?"

"How can I not be back there? They weren't written by Teddy. Or by anyone outside the house. Otherwise, how would they have gotten into her desk?"

"I hate to say this, but we only know they were in her desk because Scott told us that's where he found them."

I sighed loudly. "You're not helping, Seth."

He chuffed into the phone. "Sorry. Trying to do what you do. Covering all the bases."

"How can I call myself a detail person if I feel like I'm missing something obvious here?"

"There's got to be a piece of the puzzle that you don't have yet. That's all."

"Well, we got this whole puzzle from Scott, so how can we possibly get any more pieces?"

"A-ha!" Seth said. "We can go back to Scott and just ask him. Right?"

"What do you mean? What are you saying?"

"I'm saying we need to talk to Scott again. But we go to him assuming that he's not responsible. That he hasn't done anything wrong."

"In other words, the same way we went to him the other day."

"Yup, exactly. You can then tell him what you found in these manuscripts and maybe he'll be able to fill in some of the gaps about them. Maybe he just didn't tell you everything he knows. We were kind of ready to get out of there that day and maybe we rushed him and he just dumped those stacks of paper on you and let you go, assuming you'd read them and get back to him anyway."

"Good plan. I like this plan. I can get behind this plan."

I had stood up in the middle of what Seth had been saying, and now I was eagerly pacing the living room, with Vlad tottering along behind me, thinking something exciting was about to happen. He was going to be mighty disappointed when he found out I was going to get off this phone, throw on my shoes, and head out the door to Scott's house... all without him.

"I SEE," I SAID, REPEATING MYSELF for the third time in as many minutes. "No, that's fine. I get it."

I was sitting in Scott and Charlotte's living room, on the couch, with Scott seated in his La-Z-Boy recliner across the room. Teddy was in school. He wanted to go back earlier than Scott would have preferred, but everyone had urged Scott to let Teddy decide if he was ready to go back to school after the death of his mother. Scott was still taking time off work, still in the throes of dealing with the odd sorts of fallout that come when a close family member dies unexpectedly. Especially a famous one.

I had told him what I was thinking about the two novel manuscripts he had given me. I was clear that I didn't think these stories were up to Charlotte's usual standards, that I barely made sense of the beginnings of them and gave up on each one after only a hundred pages or so. I asked him again where he had found them, and he clearly and distinctly repeated what he had told me then: that he had found them in a desk drawer at the desk where Charlotte had done most of her writing.

"And you can't find digital copies of them on her computer anywhere?"

"Not anywhere that makes any sense, no. If she meant to hide them on her computer, she did a good job, Maggie."

"Plus, why would she bother to hide the digital copies and then put two big printouts in her desk drawer where anyone could find them?" I mused.

"Exactly."

"So, if Charlotte didn't write these—and I see no reason to keep believing that she did—then who else might have written them?"

He shook his head and lowered the foot rest on the recliner, putting his feet flat on the floor. "Honestly, Maggie, I have absolutely no idea. I just assumed they were Charlotte's. I mean, they have her name on them. Both of them."

"A fair assumption then. Did you read either of them?"

"No. I... couldn't. Once I found them and realized they were manuscripts, and with titles I'd never seen before, I thought of you right away since you were always the first person she showed a finished manuscript to."

"You mean, after the beta readers. She had beta readers, right?"

"Beta what?"

"Beta readers. Usually fellow writers or close friends who read your manuscript for you and help you over the rough patches early on. Plot holes or character issues. Stuff like that. Stuff I, as a proofreader, don't typically do. That's what a developmental editor does once you get the story the way you want it."

He was nodding and trying to keep up with me. I knew he wasn't all that involved in the details of Charlotte's career, even if he had been otherwise supportive. His job as a power plant worker kept him busy enough, and although he and Charlotte loved each other, they were different personality types with different skill sets. Complementary, I'd call it. At any rate, he obviously didn't know much about how Charlotte got her stories from her head into print, so I was going to have to walk him through this a little bit.

"So, you're saying," he continued, interrupting me and saving me from having to go into too much more detail, "that these two stories hadn't yet made it to the beta readers. Would that explain it? Why they weren't ready?"

He was following me all right, but he still wasn't getting it.

"Not exactly, no. Neither of these stories is internally consistent. In a lot of spots they just don't make any sense. The wording is beyond awkward. It's just... *off*."

"You keep saying that, Maggie, but you don't say how."

"Well, I brought them back so you can take a look at them yourself."

He waved a hand in my direction. "No, no. I don't want to see those right now. Not... not for a while yet. I'm... I'm not ready." He closed his eyes and exhaled, rubbing his palm on his legs and otherwise looking mighty uncomfortable.

"I'm sorry. I didn't mean to make you feel uncomfortable."

"It's okay. I just figured by handing those two stories over to you that I wouldn't have to expose myself to them just yet. That by the time you got done with them—reading them, or proofreading them, or whatever—I'd be a little bit better and might be able to talk to you about them. About what to do with them. Next, I mean."

He was having a lot of trouble getting his thoughts together and expressing them. I could see the pain and anguish. Whatever misgivings I had about him coming into this impromptu meeting, they were gone now. There was no way Scott had had anything to do with Charlotte's murder. I felt confident about that, and I was going to tell Helga as soon as I could, to prevent any rumors about Scott from taking hold. Helga wasn't exactly a gossip but I hadn't thought to extract a promise from her not to discuss what we had talked about at dinner. Better to make sure she knew not to spread bits of information that only she was privy to right now.

"Well, Scott, I honestly don't think these are in the right stage for proofreading. First I'd want to know why they read so oddly. Along with that is any information we can get about who wrote these, or, if it was indeed Charlotte, why she wrote them so cryptically."

He was nodding again, following along, but his heart wasn't in this conversation. He just wanted it to be over, and I couldn't say that I blamed him, really. I hadn't gotten any definitive answers or any new bits of information about the manuscripts, but I got what I needed to know: Scott Collins had not killed his wife, no matter what Helga had decided. And for now, that was good enough for me. I could rest a little more easily knowing that my friend Charlotte was not killed by her supposedly loving husband.

Whether or not he had penned the weird stories I still had in my possession was a completely different matter.

Chapter 10

FOR THE FIRST TIME IN MANY YEARS, I dug out my wooden tabletop editor's desk and set it up on the work table in my home office. It unfolded and could be set at just about any angle I wanted, so I could keep the pages I was working on at the right position to see clearly without squinting. The wooden adjustable lip at the bottom held the pages in place, not allowing them to cascade onto the floor or into my lap.

And, the contraption was wide enough to accommodate two sets of pages: those I still had to look at and those I had already scribbled on. This editor's desk had been a staple of my work environment for quite a few years when everyone was still working in hard copy. Sometimes I missed working like that—actual red pens on actual crisp paper, reference books like the latest dictionary and the *Chicago Manual of Style* on either side of me. I'd long since moved to editing and proofreading onscreen, with either the word processor's Track Changes feature or cyber-scribbling on PDFs with the mouse imitating the scrawl of a red pen. It was more efficient—emailing completed projects was cheaper and faster than boxing up reams of paper and toting them off to the post office to send back to the publisher at a snail's pace. It was more portable—I could essentially work anywhere I could bring a laptop. But I found that sometimes small things got missed when working exclusively on a computer screen. Perhaps it was the backlighting irritating the eyes after too long. Perhaps it was not engaging the fingers and hands in quite the same way as working with a real pen and paper. Or maybe it was just that my middle-aged brain was still adjusting to the brave new digital world. After all, I'd spent far longer with pen and paper than I'd spent so far working onscreen.

Still, it felt good and right to dig out the editor's desk for this project. If indeed it was a project. Scott had pulled back from asking me to officially proofread these two manuscripts for possible future publication once he heard me clearly state that they just weren't of publishable quality. But whether I was officially on the clock with this project or not, I felt compelled to look more closely at both of them on my own, and Scott didn't seem to have any problem allowing me to hold on to both manuscripts for a little while longer.

It was obvious to me that they made him feel uncomfortable and that he was more interested in getting them off his own radar and onto someone else's. I didn't promise him anything, and I was clear that I wouldn't be proofreading these like I did previous novels from Charlotte. I just wanted to read through them more slowly, to see if I could pick up on any patterns anywhere, somehow, that might shed some light on what was going on.

The second manuscript stayed on the dining room table for now. I had this first one set up on the editor's desk on the right side, the many pages held upright by the wooden lip at the bottom of the angled desk. I swung the goose neck lamp's bulb just over the pages so I could see them clearly. Two red-ink Pilot fine-point pens lay alongside the desk, ready for service. I picked up the first one, checked the ink level, and bent over the pages in front of me. Time to try to unlock the mysteries of Charlotte's brain.

I BARELY HEARD THE CELL PHONE RING from the other room an hour later. I had it set to go to voice mail after four rings, and I had apparently missed at least the first two rings because once I leapt up from the chair and dashed down the short hallway to the living room area where the phone was, I had missed the call. A quick glance at the screen told me it was a call from Annie, so I waited a few seconds to see if she would leave a message, and sure enough, a new voice mail alert dinged onto the main screen of the phone not long after that. It was just a quick message from Annie, who was away at college:

"Hi, Mom. Just talked to Seth. Seems like the two of you are in the thick of it again. Sorry to hear about your friend Charlotte. Can you keep an eye on Seth for a while? I don't like that he's getting dragged into another... *situation* like last year. Call me if you guys need anything. Bye!"

She was right. I should keep an eye on Seth to be sure he wasn't going down any dark paths in his mind while helping out Scott with those website issues. But something else popped into my brain as I listened to her message a second time. Yes, why hadn't I thought of that? Annie was a lit major. She essentially read things full time now. Lots of different things. Not just Jane Austen and Shakespeare. I thought I could perhaps ask for her opinion on these two manuscripts—as stories, as literature, for lack of a better term. She was learning how to be analytical about the things she read. Might as well see if any of that expensive college education was paying off in usable skills. I could tell from what little I had scrutinized in both stories that neither of them had the typical gore and horror that Charlotte had become famous for. The very things that Annie objected to in principle and avoided in person. These stories were impossible to categorize, an almost stream of consciousness devoid of the details that would have offended Annie's delicate sensibilities.

I could send her at least one of these two manuscripts to see what she could make of them. Whatever pattern was lurking underneath these seemingly random words and phrases was just beyond my comprehension. Maybe a new set of eyes—a pair completely unfamiliar with Charlotte's work and therefore unencumbered by preconceived notions and personal history with the author—might be just the ticket for discovering the truth about what was going on here.

I clicked on Annie's number and let the call go through. She picked it up on the second ring.

"Mom, hi!"

"Hi, sweetie. How are you? Sorry I didn't pick up the phone when you called."

"Don't tell me. Let me guess. It was out by the door and you were in your office." I could hear her laugh. My routine was a lot more routine than I had realized.

"You know me too well."

"I didn't have anything big to say or ask. Just was checking in on you and Seth. I've been reading about the Charlotte situation in the newspapers up here."

"You read newspapers?"

She sighed. "Not actual newspapers on paper, no. Websites. Always websites, Mom."

"Which papers? The *Bugle*?"

"A little. Also the student paper here. I'm close enough to home that we get big stories from Brighton up here on campus."

"And this is a big story then?" I was confirming what she said more than I was actually asking her.

"Oh, heck yeah. Murder of a local author? Sure."

"Yeah. Sometimes I forget she'd gotten quite famous with those last few novels of hers."

"Anyway, I just wanted to be sure Seth wasn't getting in over his head. I tried to ask him if he was okay, but you know Seth. He just brushed it off like it was no big deal. He didn't really want to talk about what was going on. I was just trying to make sure he wasn't clamming up again, like he did after Allen died last year."

I sighed. She was such a kind soul, though a little too sensitive for her own good. Still, I preferred to see her like this than being too callous. I was just afraid this was going to end up hurting her at some point because it exposed her to all sorts of bad people and situations. She wasn't really overly trusting, but she did tend to see the good in people who didn't deserve her gracious demeanor.

"So far he's fine. I'm keeping an eye on him, Annie. Charlotte's husband asked him to look more deeply at her website. It was hacked right before she was murdered."

"I know. That's gotta be connected then, right?"

"So it would seem. That's what both Seth and Scott think right now, anyway."

"Is that why Seth is involved? The geek coding stuff, right?"

"Apparently. He was helping Charlotte with her substandard blog site skills, so Scott just naturally asked him to look into what might have happened when the hackers got in."

"What exactly did they do?"

"Posted some nasty 'We're comin' to get you' stuff right on the main page. A little creepy when I first saw it."

"Ugh. I missed that detail in the papers somehow."

"The police aren't releasing any information about that part of the investigation. And, we helped Charlotte take it down and disabled not long after it first showed up. But then it came back."

"So the police don't think it has anything to do with her murder?"

"We're not sure, but they're not beating down Seth's door or Scott's with questions about it, that's for sure."

"That's nuts."

"I agree, honey. And it seems to be the only solid lead the police could have, if they only decided to look into it more. I don't have any other clue who might be involved in this murder. It's... vexing."

"Only you would use a word like 'vexing.'"

"Why does everybody pick on me about that word?"

"What?"

"Never mind."

"Do you think that's such a good idea, Mom?" Seth asked me, as he forked another bit of cheeseburger pie into his mouth.

Any second now he'd start making those yummy sounds he used to make as a wee toddler whenever he got a comfort food like this. Didn't matter that he was now officially in his late twenties. He'd do it. And I'd still find it endearing. It's what moms lived for sometimes.

"Yes, I do. I think Annie could give me the unique insight I need on this. I need an objective set of eyes on these stories because they're driving me crazy."

"They're just stories, Mom. Let 'em go." He was down to the last few bites of the pie and I could see his psyche warring with itself: should he wolf down those last few bites like he really wanted to do, or should he savor them more slowly and not rush through them? He'd had this same unspoken war with his inner child ever since he'd actually been a child, and I never got tired of watching it. I was pretty sure he didn't even realize he was doing it. Still, I watched.

"That's half the point, though, Seth," I countered. "They don't seem like stories. They don't read like stories. Not really."

"Then what are they? Exactly?"

"Not sure. That's why I think Annie might be able to help. After all, she's learning how to decipher pieces of literature from the inside, isn't she?"

He choked a bit on his cheeseburger pie. "Is she? Like, is that even a life skill that she can ever earn money with? Like, ever?"

"Knock it off. This isn't the time to get into that old argument."

Seth had chosen not to go to college. At first I'd been a little reticent about his choice, but he was supporting himself fine the past few years and he was always a few steps ahead of the digital age into which he and his sister had been born, so I no longer worried about his financial future. What he did with that money, of course, was an entirely separate issue. I saw a few too many video games in his apartment and more than one gaming console hooked up to his gigantic flat-screen television. I said nothing. He had no wife, no children, and as far as I knew he was paying his bills without the help of either of his parents. What more could a parent ask in these days of economic uncertainty? And it's not like the internet and computers were going to go away anytime soon, so Seth was going to have steady income into the foreseeable future. That is, unless we ended up in that zombie apocalypse he was so fond of reading about and watching on that big screen television. I myself wasn't partial to seeing zombified dead flesh four feet wide on a wall of my own domicile, but hey... different strokes for different folks, right?

Annie, on the other hand, had always had a hankering for the more elegant and lovely things of this world. College had been a given for her from a very early age, and her choice of major so far had borne out her personality quite logically. I wasn't going to argue with her about the financial logic behind majoring in English literature. She was also learning how to live life, how to interact with other adult human beings, and how to think logically about deeper issues. What was that sort of learning worth? Well, I was going to find out eventually after Annie graduated, but that was still most of a school year away. Right now she was happy on campus and loved her studies. And, her grades told her father and me that she was good at this, so we weren't complaining.

And her skills as a deep thinker, as someone trained to look into a work of fiction, were perhaps what I was lacking as I kept reading parts of these stories and coming up with nothing to tell me what was going on. I only hoped that Annie would not need to know anything about Charlotte's other, published work in order to help me out, because she definitely would not want to start reading that stuff, even in the name of helping her mother.

"So, do you think she *will* help you out?" Seth's question brought me back to reality.

"Yup. She said she'll come home this weekend and I'll give her the manuscripts then."

"You'll probably ply her with her favorite foods all weekend in an effort to get her to commit to reading them both."

"I would do no such thing."

He guffawed. "What do you think *this* is all about? Cheeseburger pie? I have it on very good authority that you don't make this unless you know I'm going to be here."

I smiled. "You caught me."

I wasn't sure a mother's skills in providing comfort food would ever get old. I was pretty sure that, even once Seth or Annie knew what I was doing, they'd still come around for some of the favorites they didn't want to bother cooking for themselves. They'd say I was making it with love or some other such rot, to compliment me and stroke my maternal ego, but of course it was mostly about them being too lazy and too cheap to make the stuff themselves. I'd noticed a long time ago that neither of them had extravagant tastes when it came to their favorite homemade foods from Mom. Certainly nothing they *couldn't* make themselves. They simply chose to wait till they were home again, where I would make their favorites without even being asked.

And as for what I got in return? Besides that warm fuzzy feeling that all mothers adored when their kids were enjoying something homemade? Well, we also got whatever we were trying to barter for in the first place, of course. Worked every time, and I wasn't too proud to admit it.

"So, once she's here, you're going to fill her full of your crazy ideas *and* full of... what, exactly?"

"Oh, Seth, I know darned well you're asking me because if it's something you like, you'll conveniently show up and confiscate some of it yourself." I grinned at him.

"*Moi?*"

"Ha!" I snorted. "Yes, you. If you show up this weekend when Annie is here, it won't be because you miss her so terribly. I'm not an idiot, you know."

"Seriously, though, what are you going to make for her? I... um... just want to see if it's the kind of food that will work. I don't want you to waste your time and effort making something that she might not find tempting enough."

"You're such an altruistic brother and son."

"Hey, what can I say? I love my sister like she was my... sister."

"The brotherly love is simply oozing out of your pores. I can almost see it hitting the floor from over here. Nice."

"Thanks. I try."

"Anyway, I was thinking I'd start with homemade macaroni and cheese."

"The kind that gets crusty around the edges of the pan?"

"Is there any other kind?"

"Not worth mentioning, no."

"True enough. Then maybe for breakfast on Saturday morning I'll make homemade monkey bread."

"Geez, yer killing me here. Monkey bread? I don't even warrant monkey bread when I stay over."

"That's because I almost never need a big favor out of you. Plus, you live five miles away."

"Fair enough."

And with that we got back to the serious business of scarfing down the rest of the cheeseburger pie. I was beginning to regret not having made a second one to reheat later.

Chapter 11

"YOU HAVE GOT TO BE KIDDING ME!" Annie exclaimed when I had finished filling her in on what I was hoping to get her to do for me.

"No! Of course I'm not kidding. Whatever would make you think I'm kidding?" I was pretty sure I hadn't sounded like I was joking, but sometimes those twenty-two years between us made a really huge difference in perception.

"Mom, I have purposely avoided *anything* that woman has written ever since you first told me about her. And *now* you're asking me to read not one, but *two* of her manuscripts on purpose? Things that haven't even been vetted by an editor yet, or even read by *you*?"

"Well, I looked through them both a little bit. Annie, honey, I'm reasonably sure there's nothing in either of these manuscripts that would offend you or upset you. That's part of my problem with them, actually."

"And how could that be a problem?" She was standing across the living room, her hands on her hips, her lips pressed tightly together. This wasn't going as well as I had hoped.

"Not a problem like that!" I sighed and sat on the couch, my head in my hands. Suddenly, one English major was talking to another and we couldn't communicate a single solid idea back and forth. The irony was not lost on me.

"Then exactly what *is* the problem, Mom?"

"The problem is that there are complete manuscripts here that don't make much sense as stories, but I suspect there is something else going on underneath these 'stories.' The one I looked at is a hot mess. I thought maybe you could help me decipher whatever is buried here. You'd be a fresh set of eyes that wouldn't have the bias, the preconceived notions I might have as Charlotte's longtime proofreader. That's all. I just thought you'd have the training to help me out."

"Training?"

"As an English literature major, of course."

"I... don't even have my degree yet, though, Mom."

"Well, it's not like I'm asking you to perform heart surgery here. This is more like a little amateur sleuthing, that's all. Your eyes are kind of being trained to read a story and pick apart whatever is going on underneath, thematically."

"You think there's something going on... underneath thematically?"

I nodded. "I do. Yes."

She sighed and plopped down on the easy chair across the room from me.

"What does that even mean?"

"You're the one going to college for this stuff, not me! Doesn't what I'm saying make any sense to you at all?"

She frowned and cast her gaze at the floor.

"Yes?" I said, tentatively. I didn't like the eerily quiet tone she had suddenly adopted.

"I think you'd better sit down."

"Sweetie, I already am sitting down. See?" I gestured to my lap as I sat on the couch, then started drumming my fingers on my thighs, subconsciously holding my breath and waiting for her to speak.

"Then I think you'd better *stay* sitting down."

"Okay, still sitting. What's up?"

By this point, I'd completely forgotten about Charlotte and her manuscripts. I had a funny feeling that this had nothing at all to do with Charlotte, or even Annie's reticence to read these two manuscripts.

"Let's just say I'm not an English major anymore."

She looked up from the floor then and tried out a sheepish little smile on me, which mostly worked, except that her father and I were paying a ton of money to keep her in college. I didn't know where she was taking me next, but I sat there hoping and praying that she wasn't about to tell me that she had dropped out of school.

"I think I dropped out of school."

To say I had a few Zen moments of parental silence as I stared at her from across my living room is putting it mildly. I had absolutely no clue what to say to her about this, but at least that kept me from saying something stupid or angry... or whatever this emotion was that I was feeling. I just knew I didn't like it very much.

I took a few more deep breaths—but not too deep or I might pass out—and closed my eyes, willing myself to remain calm and clearheaded no matter what Annie said next.

"Okay, sweetie," I said, slowly, eyes still closed. I could hear her fidgeting on the easy chair, tapping on something and saying absolutely nothing. That was probably wise. "Tell me exactly what you mean by 'dropped out of school.'"

"Well," she said, sounding hesitant and like a young girl again, "I don't mean *completely* out of school. Don't get too upset."

"How can you drop only *partly* out of school?" I countered quickly—probably too quickly—opening my eyes and staring at her while I waited for whatever backpedaling she was about to do.

"Because I didn't completely leave the whole school."

"That's not a heck of a lot clearer. You know that, right?"

I was pretty sure I looked upset, so I stopped trying to rein in the facial expressions. Best to rein in the speech patterns and voice modulation instead. The facial expressions were too many things to control on top of the raw emotion that had just welled up unbidden.

"I mean, I just dropped out of the English department. Out of the humanities program."

I blinked. I waited. I said nothing. There was probably some punch line, something that would wrap up her little bombshell into a better package than she had just handed me a moment before. That package was still ticking and felt like it could go off at any moment, so I tried to wait patiently for her to fill me in.

"For an English major, you sure aren't being very clear in your word choices right now, little missy."

"Okay, Mom, now I know you're mad. You haven't called me 'little missy' since that time I accidentally spilled nail polish on the dining room table."

"And I'm about as happy with you now as I was then. What brought this on?" I folded my arms across my chest, with all the negative body language I could muster, and decided to say very little until she had gotten everything out. I had been wrong about a thing or two before, and I didn't want to lash out at Annie before I was sure she had done something that warranted it. And the jury on that was still out.

"I just wasn't feeling it in the English department."

I closed my eyes again. This wasn't going to be as straightforward as I had hoped. "I have no idea what that means but I'm quite sure you're going to find a way to tell me. Right?"

"Mom, I didn't see much point in staying in the English department. So, I dropped out and moved over to the engineering department."

"The what?"

"The engineering department. You heard me." She was frowning at me now, and I regretted having opened my eyes again.

"Why on God's green earth would you, of all people, transfer to the engineering department?"

"Because I like it. Because I'm good at it."

"You're what?"

"I'm good at it. I figured out last year that I was getting my best grades in my science and math classes and that I was paying attention in them more than in my English classes. Those were starting to feel lame and boring."

I frowned at her.

"No offense, Mom."

"None taken. Why would I be offended?"

"Because you were an English major. I don't mean that it's boring for everyone, but it was getting really boring for me."

She was looking at me quite sincerely, and I found I had absolutely nothing to say. What could I say, after all? It's not like she was telling me she had murdered the neighbors or pulled the wings off flies. She was just switching majors—from English to engineering. Hey, they both even started with the same three letters. How bad could it be, after all?

"Mom, are you all right?"

"I'm fine. Why do you ask?"

"Because you look a little... clammy. Are you sure you're all right? You're not going to faint, are you?"

"Why would I faint just because my daughter is abandoning me?"

Annie rolled her eyes at me and sighed exaggeratedly. "Mom!"

"Okay, perhaps I'm overreacting a little. But, I just didn't see this coming at all. Not. At. All."

"I know. Neither did I, really. But once I figured out why I was so unhappy, then everything sort of fell into place."

"And... this is a done deal already? You've spoken to the English department?"

"Actually, I spoke to the engineering department first, to make sure I could transfer there. Didn't want to burn any bridges or anything. Right?"

I nodded. "Of course, of course. Makes sense to do it in that order." I was still nodding, letting this all sink in.

I just hadn't ever envisioned my sensitive, Shakespeare-reading daughter as an engineer. Like, not at all.

"Then I went to the head of the English department and told them what had happened, what I wanted to do."

"And?"

"And they gave me the paperwork to fill out, and there I was, out of the humanities school and into the engineering department."

"Even though you're already a senior?"

"Well..."

I sat up straight, having been lulled into a false sense of security. "Well what?"

"Now, Mom, lower your radar. It's not all that bad..."

"What isn't all that bad?"

"You sound like you're about to call me 'little missy' again. Seriously, Mom, calm down before you blow a gasket."

"Do you even know what a gasket is?" I sighed loudly.

"No, but I'm betting I'll know more about what it is than you do within the next few years."

"Few *years*? What exactly does that mean?"

"Well, I might have to redo a few credits here and there because I switched majors so drastically."

"And so late," I added helpfully.

"And so late, yes. Thank you, Mom, for pointing that out. I was just getting to that part."

"The part where you have to stay in school longer to get through a degree?"

"Mom, you're not helping."

"I know I'm not. That's not really my job right now."

"What *is* your job right now then? To make me feel bad about my choices? The choices that make the most sense to me?"

I bit my lip and kept myself from saying the bajillion things I really wanted to say right now. A few years ago I had taped a piece of paper to my computer monitor that said simply, "You can't unsay it." It had become a sort of battle cry for me in the brave new online world.

I figured the battle cry would serve me well right now in person too, so I said nothing and waited for Annie to continue.

"Mom, I didn't do this to make you mad. Or to piss off Dad. I did this because it's what I want to do with my life."

I nodded. She was right, of course. Even if it had taken her three years of college—expensive college—to figure it out, at least she *had* figured it out, which was kind of the point of post-secondary schooling anyway, wasn't it?

"Let's face it. An English degree wasn't going to get me a great job unless I wanted to teach or write."

"And you don't want to do either of those."

"You know I don't. I'm not extroverted enough to teach, and I'm not an introvert like you so I'd never survive being a writer, either. And being a full-time permanent scholar does *not* appeal to me in the least."

Actually, I had always thought she might enjoy being a professional student, but I was relieved to hear her father and I wouldn't be supporting her ongoing credit habit into her forties after all.

"And so, math and science and engineering it is, then?"

She nodded. "Uh huh. I start in January."

"What type of engineering? Have you decided?"

She nodded again. "I'm pretty sure I'm leaning toward electrical engineering."

I nodded in response. There was a hell of a lot of nodding going on in my living room. I half expected to see Vlad start nodding, but he was calmly snoozing on the rug in the center of the room, blissfully unaware of the subtleties of college majors and any concepts of electrical engineering or the noble themes of English literature.

"Well," I said finally, "that's great then. Really. You can rewire the apartment for me once you graduate. I keep tripping breakers if I try to use my printer when the air conditioner is running in my office." I smiled, hoping to indicate that a truce flag was waving.

Annie let out a long sigh and smiled, sitting back down on the easy chair. "They'll send you the updated invoice once this semester is over."

"Updated invoice?" I asked, rather quietly. This didn't seem like something I wanted to hear right now.

"You know, because I have to do another three years in order to catch up on all the courses I missed while I was still an English major."

She had tried to say this as casually as possible, obviously hoping that I wouldn't put two and two together and get four. But, even though I had been an English major, I could do at least that much math in my head.

"All the courses you missed?"

"Uh huh," she said airily, not meeting my gaze across the room.

"All. The courses. You. Missed."

"Mm hmm." Now she was avoiding my gaze *and* trying to sound as if she hadn't gotten my suspicions up.

"And what exactly does that mean for us as your parents? Your tuition-paying parents, I mean?"

"Not much. Just a few more years of tuition so I can get the engineering degree."

"A few more years..."

"Uh huh." She was gazing at her manicured nails as if they were works of art.

"Of tuition..."

"Yeah."

"And room and board," I added, in case she had somehow forgotten that she would still need to eat and sleep for these extra three years.

"Well, of course, room and board too," she said, smiling beatifically.

"I don't know, Annie. I think you should have transferred to the drama department. You're quite the little actress."

"Actress?"

"Don't play coy with me, little missy."

"Mom."

"Just wait until your father gets home."

"Mom, he doesn't live here anymore, remember?"

"I meant, wait till he gets home to his own house. He's footing half the bill here too, as you might recall. And he's a lot more of a skin flint than I am, if that's even humanly possible."

She was frowning again, the cherubic smile completely gone.

"You're not going to tell him right away, are you?"

"Ha!" I said, laughing for the first time in this never-ending conversation. "Not right away, no. In fact, not at all."

She smiled. "You're not going to tell him at all?"

"No, I'm certainly not."

"That's awesome!"

"*You* are."

IN A SORT OF QUID PRO QUO, Annie offered to read the two manuscripts anyway. She knew she was going to be in dutch with both of her parents, and an easy way to get me to not seethe at her was to placate me by saying yes to my initial request. Smart girl. But of course, anyone majoring in engineering was smart, right? It was going to take me a little bit of time to get used to the idea of my baby girl being an electrical engineer, but I supposed I would get over it. Apparently I still had *three years* to get used to it. And I was going to get my way with the manuscripts after all... without having to make macaroni and cheese or monkey bread. Win-win.

Annie and I sat next to each other at my small dining room table, with the first manuscript spread out before us. I was trying to show her the odd phrases and whole paragraphs that had stumped me when I had first read them. She nodded a lot and kept flipping a few pages, first forward, then back again.

"If you don't mind taking a look while you're here this weekend I'd really appreciate it."

She put her arm around me and scooted her chair a little closer. "Mom, anything for you."

"Anything except saving me a little of my hard-earned money."

"Mom."

"What?"

She sighed. "Nothing."

I was going to have fun milking this for all the guilt it was worth. It might even end up being worth what I was going to be paying for it. Probably not, but it might.

I pointed to a section of text on one of the pages spread out in front of us. "See how this entire paragraph just seems to read like it's not even a story at all?" I said, pointing to something in the middle of a page that was barely prose, let alone good fiction.

She read the section silently, nodding throughout. "I see it, yeah. It reads like... well, I don't know *what* it reads like. Nothing, really. Like a lot of nothing."

She started flipping back and forth some more, further into the manuscript, then all the way toward the end. "I'm not even seeing the same character names back here as I saw in the beginning."

"That's precisely the sort of thing I mean."

"Is this maybe some sort of anthology of shorter stories then?"

"I don't think so. Right about here"—I flipped almost to the tail end of the stack of papers—"she comes back to the two main names she was using in the very beginning. I can't make out why she would do that, though."

"Have you read the whole thing then?"

I shook my head. "No, I'm afraid not. It started to really bother me once I realized I wasn't reading it like a proofreader and I wasn't reading like a reader, either. I was reading it like... well... like..."

"Like a detective," she interjected.

"Yes. Like a detective."

"A detective who happens to be a proofreader."

I turned to look at her, puzzled. "What does that mean?"

"It means your attention to detail is going to be the death of you."

She was smiling but I couldn't find it in me to smile just now. "Gosh, I hope not. Look what happened to poor Charlotte."

"Oh, geez. I'm sorry, Mom. I didn't mean that! It was just a figure of speech."

"I know. It's fine."

"You might want to be careful, though. If these are connected to whatever happened to Charlotte, this could be scary."

"I don't necessarily think they're connected. I just think they're... well, weird. That's all. I wasn't thinking about the murders, per se."

"Then what were you thinking about?"

"Just that... well, that something is going on underneath all of this stuff, this investigation. I just don't have a clue what it is or even what direction to look in first. It's like there's too much loose information out there about Charlotte, about what was going on with her and her writing, and I don't have one single idea what any of it means."

"Ah, I see. But, they could all be related, right? I mean, I'm not completely out in left field, am I?"

"No, you're not. Anything is possible, sweetie. Anything."

"Oh goody," she said, grinning cheerily and reaching for the second manuscript.

I had a feeling she didn't mean that one little bit.

Chapter 12

I REALIZED A FEW HOURS AFTER ANNIE HAD CRASHED in my office on the daybed that I had overreacted to her news about switching to the engineering department at her school. If I was completely objective about it, I was acting opposite to the way most parents would have acted hearing that one of their children wanted to be an engineer rather than... well, than whatever you could be with a degree in English literature. Right out of college, in this day and age, that job probably included saying things like, "Would you like fries with that?" I would have to remember to apologize to Annie in the morning.

Tonight, though, I was hoping to find out more about Charlotte and her writing. Sure, I knew what they were like on the inside since I had read every single one of them as a proofreader. But, since they were a tad too gory for my personal tastes, I had never joined a Facebook group of her fans or subscribed to her website or anything like that. I didn't know much about her fans, though I was now a lot more curious about them than I had been. After all, one of them could have conceivably killed her. The very notion that someone out there in the great fandom of Charlotte Collins could have done something so heinous made me sick to my stomach, but I had to press on and see if I could find any connections among her many fans. Some connection that might lead to solving her murder.

I started with a trip back to her website. Seth must have disabled it again because the hacker's ominous words were no longer visible— thank God—so the site was less scary than it had been. I clicked on the About link and began to read through everything I could find on her site. None of this was particularly new, since I had proofread the text for her ages ago when the site first went live. Plus, she liked to run any new content by me first to make sure she hadn't missed any glaring errors or typos. So, I read through each hot link and tabbed my way across the main menu along the top of the screen. When I got to the tab marked Other Fan Resources, though, I hesitated. This was where I hoped to find links to other places on the internet where Charlotte's books were discussed, where her fans gathered. It made me nervous. *Click.*

Most of the links at the top of this tabbed page were links to her official satellite pages elsewhere: Facebook, Twitter, Instagram, even Pinterest. Seems Charlotte had been everywhere a savvy modern writer needed to be in order to satisfy her fans. I clicked through to each of these pages and groups and either joined the group or followed the page, whatever was required. A little bit of looking around in each spot didn't turn up anything gravely suspicious, so I continued on, letting my clicks from Charlotte's site open up new browser tabs to take me to each link. And although some of the fans on each of these other sites had odd quirks easily discerned by reading their obnoxious (and poorly spelled and punctuated) posts, still nothing sounded quite so outrageous as to give me pause.

I gave up after an hour of random clicking and reading, finally heading to Google to see what links her name brought up. A few short clicks and I was staring at a screen full of links to all sorts of fan sites and discussion forums and subforums centered around the works of Charlotte Collins. I wasn't sure whether to be thrilled that there would be plenty of opportunity to read things from all sorts of fans or to be overwhelmed by the thought of reading through so many sites, so many pages, so many forums, so many posts... so many *words*. Unless I quickly found something that was clearly suspicious, I was going to have my work cut out for me. And, if I had been absolutely certain that the culprit was a fan, a reader, then I would have dived in and not worried about lost time and effort. But it was clear that I could easily end up swimming in a vast sea of words (poorly spelled and punctuated words) with no hope of coming up for air and breathing again.

Still, I saw no other options in front of me—not at one o'clock in the morning, at least—so I bookmarked the Google search and clicked on the first major link.

"Might as well jump in with both feet," I mumbled to myself.

"Whuh?" I startled awake and sat bolt upright in my chair. I'd somehow dozed off while reading a blog about Charlotte's books. No single blog post, mind you. An entire blog. This fan had actually started an entire blog to talk about all the gory and not-so-gory stuff. I had been reading entry after entry, wondering if this person was a total freak and capable of doing harm to his favorite author. Of course, to those of us who *weren't* psychotic, it seemed unthinkable that one could harm a person who had become so important to you. You had to be a special kind of creepy to look at a person whose work you admired and turn around and kill that person. Was the person who had taken the time to write all of these blog posts the same sort of person who could kill the very object of those posts? I had read nearly all of his entries while I was asking myself that very question, over and over again. But I had not gotten to the answer before nodding off on my computer keyboard. Apparently my face had hit the keyboard at just the right angle to start typing the letter S over and over again onto a reply window on his blog post, the one I had been reading when I nodded off. And somehow I had just now startled awake, only to discover a million S's in that reply window and some saliva that had seeped out of the corner of my mouth and onto the keyboard. Lovely. I certainly was a charming creature when I was tired.

I got up and headed for the bathroom, where I retrieved a few wet wipes out of the dispenser I kept under the bathroom sink in the vanity and traipsed back to my office. I swiped the keyboard as thoroughly as I could with the wet wipes and hoped it would survive.

I looked again at the blog post I had been reading when I dozed off. I was almost done reading every single entry, and I hadn't gotten any closer to discovering whether or not he could have ended Charlotte's life. What hadn't occurred to me before I started to read—for hours and hours, I might add—was that it would have been smart to check where this person was writing from. So, now I was awake enough to think straight, and I rubbed my face and tried to even out the indentations made on my left cheek from the letters A, S, D, and F. Plus, I thought, a little bit of Z and X, too. The feeling was starting to come back into my face in sections, and they all were tingling.

Now I was definitely awake, but I wasn't any closer to finding out what I wanted to know. One click on the Contact tab of this guy's website and I saw what I had not wanted to see: he was writing from Australia. He was about as far from being local as a person could get. I had just spent the past few hours reading post after post of barely interesting glimpses into this man's brain, hoping to find something to use, only to find out he was on the other side of the world and couldn't possibly have killed anyone here in Brighton. Lesson learned.

Time wasted, yes. But time to move on, too. I had no idea what I was doing or how I was going to find what I was looking for. In fact, maybe I was so far off base that I should give up and let the local police do their job. Just because Scott had become a little frustrated with their lack of progress didn't meant there was nothing happening on that front. They just weren't sharing it with Scott, or with anyone else. I would have to find a way to tell Scott that there might not be anything for us to find after all.

But that was going to have to wait till morning. I was exhausted and I needed to lie my head on a soft pillow and hope the key-shaped indentations in my face had faded by the time I had to get up and face a new day. Plus, I really didn't want to have to try to explain to Annie why my face looked like a keyboard in reverse topography.

I WOULD BE THE FIRST PERSON TO ADMIT that my life was small. And I would also be the first person to admit that I kind of liked it that way. I was a creature of routine. I craved sameness. I craved habits and predictability in all things. I was about as far from being adventurous as a person could get without being declared legally dead. But somehow, amid a personality as firmly rooted in dullness as last year's favorite doll for children at Christmas, I had begun to obsess about this situation with Charlotte. At the moment I was torn between siding with Scott and thinking that the police weren't doing their job, and siding with the police in their unspoken suspicion of Scott as the stereotypical murder suspect/spouse. I was starting to waffle so much I needed some syrup.

And frankly, if I hadn't been handed these two curious manuscripts, I would now be thinking Scott was the most likely suspect. Then a part of me started to think, "That's absurd. Scott and Charlotte have always had a smooth, loving marriage." That's when I realized that I must have watched too many bad television movies and bad cop dramas. Too many stories where the silent, quiet neighbor turns out to be a psychopath, where the loving marriage is really a horror show of abuse and dysfunction.

I had to face facts: I had absolutely no idea what to think or who to accuse. It was time to start getting my ducks in a row and figure out exactly what I knew for sure, and what I merely *thought* I knew. Plus, a few things I definitely did not know. Well, perhaps more than a few of those things.

I grabbed my morning cup of coffee and tiptoed back to my office, where Annie was still sacked out on the daybed I kept in there for when either she or Seth needed a place to crash. I had lucked out so far in that I'd never had to house both of them at the same time, because my choice of this small two-bedroom apartment had been the right one at the time but sometimes really cramped my style. I had to curtail some of my rampant book purchases in the past year because I had essentially run out of shelf space... and run out of places to put more shelves. If I were smart, I would start looking for a three-bedroom apartment when my lease came up for renewal. I knew firsthand that sometimes one's adult children still needed a safe haven with at least one of their parents. Seth had been my "problem child" in that department in years past, although at the moment both Annie and Seth were out on their own. Annie was away at college and was hoping to get her own apartment off campus when the school year ended. And since it was clear she was going to be at that school for a few extra years, she might actually be out from under both of her parents for good now. But, for this particular weekend, she was here with me, so I could fill her full of Mom's food and hugs in exchange for some advice on what to think about those two blasted manuscripts.

So, I tiptoed back to the office, hoping to sneak in, grab those manuscripts, and sit with them in the living room while I sipped some hot java. I could let her sleep in as long as she liked. Maybe just reading them, rather than trying to automatically decipher them, would help me absorb whatever secrets they held. Wasn't it always the way, that as soon as you stopped striving over a problem and obsessing about it, the solution came to you? That's precisely what I was hoping.

I turned the doorknob as slowly and silently as I could, but the door always clicked when it opened, and this time was no different. I quietly pushed the door open—at least it didn't squeak anymore now that I had taken the time to spritz some WD-40 on it last month—and eased into the room, looking around for the two manuscripts. Ah! There they were on the small end table I had put next to the daybed. She had stacked them there haphazardly, one on top of the other, and the top manuscript no longer had the large binder clip holding its pages together. It sat precariously, ready to cascade onto the floor with the slightest breeze.

Annie's hand was outside the quilt, looking almost as if she was reaching out for the stack of pages balanced on the end table. I drew in my breath as I saw her hand move slightly while she slept. I doubled my tiptoeing speed and lunged for the papers before she inadvertently knocked them all over. From what I remembered, this printout didn't even have page numbers on it, so putting the pages back together in the right order would be a complete nightmare. This was especially true because of how disjoint the story itself was, how poorly it read, how convoluted the prose was. I would never be able to figure out how to reassemble this monstrosity if those pages went flying. All I could think as I fell forward was, "Who in their right mind doesn't put page numbers on a printout of a manuscript?"

And with that, I remembered that I am perhaps the klutziest person on Earth. I lunged forward to save that top, unclipped manuscript from a disastrous flight off the end table and onto the floor. Trying to save it from a random flick of the wrist from Annie's hand, which was too close to the pile for comfort.

Of course, I tried too hard and my slippered foot caught on one small corner of the area rug in the center of the room. I pitched forward clumsily, my outstretched hand—the one that was meant to save the manuscript from tumbling—catching on the corner of the end table and just touching the top edge and corner. My hand came downward and brought the entire stack with it, of course. And, as these events so often do, everything fell into slow motion, my hand slowly pulling a bunch of pages with it. I was having that awful feeling of helplessness once a tumble starts, and because of my concern for the integrity of the stack of pages, it never occurred to me to be concerned with my own safety. Not there in my own little home office, for crying out loud.

So, even as the manuscript's pages cascaded gently and inexorably to the floor, my own clumsy self cascaded onto the carpet—well, my knees did, anyway. The top half of me then continued forward at an alarming rate, and I couldn't stop my forehead from hitting the corner of that end table with an audible *whap!* Then, a lot of things seemed to happen at once. My hand instinctively tried to break my fall, but it succeeded only in dragging even more of the loose pages onto the floor, where they briefly made contact with the back of my head and then flew off in all directions. I heard myself moaning, "Oh no! Oh no!" but, for some reason, even I wasn't sure if I was wailing about having whacked my head or about having caused all those manuscript pages to go flying, the very thing I had been trying to prevent.

In a split second I was on the area rug on my hands and knees, my forehead throbbing painfully, my eyes staring in unbelief at the carpet of white paper all around me. I was seriously screwed.

"Mom?"

Ah, and on top of it all, I had awakened Annie. Great.

"Oh, hi, honey," I said, still staring at the papers and still hovering over them on my hands and knees. "I didn't mean to wake you." I lifted one arm off the floor and touched my wounded forehead where I had whacked it on the edge of that table.

"Are you okay?" she asked and swung her legs off the side of the daybed. "You're bleeding."

I brought my hand away from my forehead and found that she was right. There was a small amount of blood on my fingertips. Great. On top of everything else, I was probably going to have a goose egg. That was going to be fun to explain to everyone I met. The good thing was that at least most of them already knew I was a complete klutz. They wouldn't have any problem stretching their imaginations enough to picture me wounding myself in my own house with one misstep. Sad, really, but there you have it.

"I'm fine, Annie. Really. I just bumped my head on the end table." I gingerly touched the wound again, making sure it wasn't bleeding profusely, and I was relieved to find that it wasn't. "I... well, let's just say your mother the klutz is alive and well."

She frowned at me as I sat back down. "Alive and well, but for how long? Geez, Mom, you need to be more careful. What if you knock yourself out sometime and nobody else is here to help you?"

"Annie, it's fine. I was actually trying to keep that loose manuscript from falling onto the floor."

She glanced at the floor full of papers. "Great job, I see."

"Don't be such a smart-ass, Annie."

"But Mom," she said, smirking at me but still eyeing the gash on my forehead, "I know how much you look forward to me being a smart-ass whenever I'm home."

"Not you, sweetheart. That's your brother's job."

We both smiled. "Let me help you pick up all these papers," she said, slipping off the daybed and onto her knees on the floor.

"No!" I said as she reached for a random group of papers. "There still might be some sort of semblance of order here in the way they fell. Don't touch them until I try to gather them back up the way they fell."

"They don't have page numbers on them?"

"Nope. Didn't you notice last night when you were looking at them?"

"Not really, no. I was too busy trying to make some sense out of them. Out of *any* of this." She spread her arms wide to take in and include all the papers across the floor.

"I don't suppose you found anything worthwhile, did you?" I wasn't going to get my hopes up, but I had to ask.

She shook her head. "No. You were right. This story is a complete mess. I'm not even sure I could call it a proper story. Unless she was experimenting with some new form of storytelling. You know, something *avant garde*. Post-modern or something like that. Know what I mean?"

I nodded. "Yeah, but I don't think Charlotte was into that sort of writing. The curious part is why this is a printout. Scott said he couldn't find any documents or other files with names that would be these stories on her computer."

"And yet it's obvious they're printouts."

"Instead of what?"

"Instead of, say, typewritten."

"On a typewriter?" I hadn't even considered that possibility.

"Well, it would have explained why they're on paper and not in the computer. But no, these aren't from any typewriter, are they?"

I reached for the intact, clipped second manuscript still on the end table. "You're right. That's definitely a laser printout of something like Arial or Helvetica. Not a typewriter. And I used to use typewriters so I would know. Plus, no typos that I can see offhand. That's pretty rare on a typewriter, even with a correction ribbon."

She took the stack of manuscript pages from me and scrutinized them herself. "You're right. I hadn't noticed that part."

"Probably because you've never had to use a typewriter."

"Thank God."

"Hey, it wasn't that bad."

"Yes, it was. You used to tell us horror stories of having to type papers for people in college for spending money. I seem to remember stories about how tough it was to leave enough room at the bottom of a piece of paper for the footnotes."

I shuddered involuntarily. "Ugh, please. I'm having PTSD flashbacks. Stop."

She giggled. "Can I please help you pick up these pages? If only so I can get out of this room and go pee?"

I glanced at the floor and realized that, indeed, the papers had spread themselves out all the way across the office from the daybed to the other end of the area rug. She would have had a terrible time trying to hop over the pile without touching or disturbing any of the papers.

"Oh, sorry." I took a quick visual inventory and decided to try to scoop up the papers all at once, hoping to coax them back into one tidier pile in the middle of the spread. If I was lucky, they would automatically fall back into line, tipping themselves in place based on the pages they were already either on top of or underneath at the edges. If I wasn't lucky, this ridiculous story would sound either more ridiculous or might actually start to make some sense.

"I take it this isn't an exact science then," said Annie, sitting cross-legged just at the foot of the daybed.

"What did I tell you about that whole smart-ass thing, young lady?"

"Right. Sorry."

After what seemed an eternity but which was probably only about thirty seconds, I managed to get the stack into some semblance of order. Of course, that only meant that the pieces of paper were all facing the same way now and weren't completely askew. Whether I had managed to get them in the right order was anybody's guess.

"Did you get them back in the right order, Mom?"

"You tell me," I said, handing her the stack and pointing to the large binder clip on the edge of the little end table. "Clip these pages back together before this happens again. I'm a total klutz and I'm making myself nervous." I chuckled, but Annie understood I meant it and quickly grabbed the binder clip and got the pages secured once more. I let out the breath I'd been holding since I had picked the pages up off the floor.

"Might not be *exactly* in the right order, but it's as close as it's going to get unless Scott can find a digital version on Charlotte's computer," I said.

"Well, for now I'm just going to put this on the end table with the other one. I gotta hit the bathroom. And then I want some of that coffee."

Annie stepped over and around me and dashed out into the hallway. I stood a little more slowly, the ol' joints singing to me as I rose.

I headed for the kitchen, hoping I had left enough coffee for Annie. Last time she was here she had preferred tea. Sometimes I couldn't keep up with the changing preferences of my grown kids. Then again, it's not like I expected them to text me whenever they changed their minds about which beverage they preferred. I would simply make another pot of coffee and hope the creamer held out all weekend.

🕷 🕷 🕷

"WHAT DO YOU SUGGEST WE DO THEN?" I asked over my second cup of coffee and her first.

"I say we ask Scott more about these documents. See if he'll let us sit and go through file names on her computer to see if anything matches up. I've read about half of that first manuscript—the one you dropped—and I could probably make a connection with a file name that has anything to do with what I read last night."

"And what did you read last night?"

"I have no idea."

I tried to laugh at this, because it was clear she meant it to be funny, but I was long past finding this situation comical.

"I'm not sure he'll let us sift through her whole computer, though. That seems a bit... intrusive."

"Maybe Seth? Would he let Seth do it?"

"Maybe. But Seth hasn't read what you've read."

"True. I hadn't thought of that."

"We should probably go talk to Scott, though. Just to see if he has any more news for us about the police investigation or anything else he might have seen or heard."

"Do you need me to come with you then?"

I could sense that she would rather stay here and use my Netflix subscription to binge-watch back episodes of *Gilmore Girls*. I was inclined to agree with her unspoken assessment of the weekend. We hadn't had good mother-daughter time in forever.

"You know, I can talk to Scott on Monday once you're back at school. Let's whip out the Netflix instead. It's such a dreary day outside."

"Do you want me to take a look at that other story, though, Mom?"

"Yeah, but it doesn't have to be right now, does it?"

She grinned at me. "Nope."

And with that, Annie skipped from the kitchen into the living room area as if she were still five years old, grabbing the television remote off the coffee table before plunking down on the couch. Vlad hopped up next to her and settled in himself. He knew a good binge-watching partner when he saw one.

Chapter 13

URING A LULL BETWEEN EPISODES, I got up from the couch and padded back to my office to retrieve one of the manuscripts. I grabbed the one on top, the one I had put back together in some semblance of order after having dropped it all over the floor. When I came back with it cradled in my arms, Annie said nothing, but she did roll her eyes at me. I also said nothing, just smiled and shrugged, and then sat back down next to her and unclipped the stack of pages. This time I wasn't reading for content or for story elements. I was simply flipping through the pages, perhaps checking to see if it felt as if they were in the right order again. Which, of course, was ridiculous since the dang thing barely made sense when I was *sure* the pages were in the right order.

Flip, flip, flip. Scan, scan, scan. Another episode was back on and Annie was completely absorbed in it, so I quietly continued to page through the stack as she watched. At one point I looked up to see what Annie was laughing at, then looked back down at the page in front of me. For some reason, my eye caught the initial letters in each line on the page, rather than trying yet again to make any sense of the words as they went across the page. And there they were. The

CHARLOTTE'S WEBSITE   **103**

words I had been looking for. The *sense* I had been looking for in these pages. Right in front of me this whole time. And of course, as soon as I wasn't trying to decipher the story, the real meaning stood out in stark relief.

I blinked, thinking that when I looked back at the page, it would be gone. But when I opened my eyes again, the words were still there. Only, they weren't going across the page like I had come to expect with every other project I had worked on, like I had always expected of every book I had ever read. The words—the words I now saw but had not seen in any conventional "reading" of these pages, came when I looked at just the first letter of each line, all the way down the page. Those first letters, when strung together, looked like this:

I AM NOT HAPPY. I HAVE NEVER BEEN HAPPY.

I drew in a big breath and tried to remain calm. Biting my lip to keep myself from crying out, I calmly turned the page and looked at the first letters on that page. The magic words continued.

SOMEONE PLEASE HELP ME. GET ME OUT.

Now I was sure. I'd been sure with the first page—too much coincidence for those words not to be deliberate—but this second page (assuming it was actually the second page and I hadn't screwed everything up by dropping the papers on the floor) clinched it for me. And it perfectly explained why the "story" itself—the words as they were strung horizontally across the pages—made so little sense. Whoever had written this had been forced to use words for each new line that started with the right letter. So, while there sometimes seemed to be a basic story idea on a few of the pages, this explained why I found the writing itself so awkward, so difficult to read... so un-Charlotte in nature.

"Mom? Are you okay?"

I blinked and looked up from the pages I held in my hands.

I then realized I had been clutching at them fiercely and flipping through them hastily. Or, at least, that must have been how it looked to my poor daughter, who looked at me as if she thought I had gone mad. And perhaps I had.

"Oh, uh, yeah. Fine, sweets. Do me a favor, though, would you?"

She frowned. "Get you a stiff drink?"

"Ha! No."

"A Valium or something?"

I shook my head. "No, I'm fine. But, take this stack of pages for a minute, would you?"

I held them out to her and she dutifully took them, looking rightfully confused. "You need to use the bathroom?"

"No, it's not that."

"Get more coffee?"

"No, not that, either. Look at the first page for me, okay?"

She looked down at the pages in her lap. "Yeah? What am I looking for exactly?"

"I need to know if it's just my imagination."

"If what's just your imagination?"

"What do you see when you look at the first letter of each line?"

"I... um... see letters. Different letters. Why do you ask?"

"I meant, look at each of those first letters and read them vertically, down the page. Just each first letter, going down the page." I held my breath as she looked down at the page again and read silently.

After a few excruciatingly long seconds, she gasped. "Mom!"

"Oh, good. So it's not just my imagination then."

"No! Certainly not! It's... amazing."

"Look at the next page. Same sort of thing there, too."

She flipped to the next page and gasped again.

"Wow! I wonder if every single page is like this." She hurriedly turned each page and glanced at those first letters, nodding as she did so. "Yeah, it keeps working. This is... wow."

I hadn't yet looked beyond that second page. "What else does it say? On those other pages?"

"Stuff like, 'I need some space,' and 'I need to talk to someone,' but that one spills onto the next page because it's too many letters to fit onto just one page."

"What are you thinking about this, Annie?"

"Probably the same two things you are," she said. "First, that I feel silly that neither of us caught this before now."

"I know, right? It's like I can't unsee it now that I've noticed it."

"How blind are we? Seriously. Both of us missed this."

"Well, to be fair, I didn't miss it today. I just missed it all the other days before this one." I grinned sheepishly.

"Yes, yes, you get the gold star, Mama. Good for you." She smiled in response. We were certainly doing a little *Gilmore Girls* bonding right about now. It felt great.

"What was the second thing you were thinking?" I asked.

"Well, obviously, that this explains why the story felt so forced. It had to be forced in order to fit these letters in, in just the right spots."

"Exactly. Only, I had a few other thoughts now that this is sinking in."

"Which are?"

"Well, that it's also clear now why this is a printout."

"It is?" She frowned.

"Sure. Computer files might restring differently depending on all sorts of things: font size, margin size, leading, other spacing, font choice. You know, all that stuff I'd look at if I was proofing a final layout. That would screw up all the letters that would appear at the beginnings of each line."

"Well, but you can hit Return and force each line to end where you want it, right?"

"Sure, but if anyone changes any of those other attributes, then your lines still break funny, probably with added short lines just before your hard return."

"And...?"

"And then you'd have some lines starting with letters that aren't part of the message you're trying to embed. The quickest way to control what a person sees—or, in our case for a while, *doesn't* see—

is to just print it out when you have it the way you want it."

"A PDF would have worked, though."

I narrowed my eyes. "You're doing that smart-ass thing again."

"But, I'm right. Why wouldn't she just create a PDF of whatever document she created to get it to look like this?"

"So, you're thinking that Charlotte wrote this? 'She'?"

"Aren't you?"

"I guess so. For the same reasons I thought it was Charlotte before. It was in her house and it probably wasn't written by Scott."

"So, is all this crying for help real then?"

"What do you mean?" I had immediately assumed it all *was* real, so this question caught me off guard.

"Well, is she—or, rather, *was* she—issuing a sort of cry for help here? Or is all of this just some sort of new storytelling technique she was trying out?"

"It sucks as a story, though."

"Well, sure, but you have to start somewhere. That might even be why it's a printout. Maybe she was going to sit with it and fix some stuff with an actual pen. I've heard rumors that some people still do that, you know." She nudged me in the ribs. She knew I still preferred to whip out that editor's desk and the Pilot fine points every once in a while.

"Smart-ass. Smart-aaassss..."

"Okay, okay. Just kidding. But not about the story thing. It's a possibility, right?"

"Of course it is."

"Especially if you're right about them having a good marriage. Her and Scott, I mean."

"I *think* I'm right, anyway. Of course, I know it's quite possible to fool everybody into thinking you have a perfectly happy relationship when, in fact, you don't."

She patted my knee, and I put my hand over hers. "So, it's possible that it really is—or, was—a cry for help?"

"I'm not sure, but I don't think we can just brush aside the idea. Not now. Not now that Charlotte is dead. And, murdered, at that."

"Well, gosh, if this really is a cry for help, then it definitely sounds as if she means she's trapped in her marriage, right? I mean, she wasn't really 'trapped' in any other way, was she? What other way could she have been trapped?"

"Maybe trapped in her publishing contract? Who knows? Maybe she still had five books to write for them, for her publishers, before they'd let her out of her contract. And they'd probably want more of the same gory genre she's been so successful with."

"Ah, I see! So maybe she was sick of writing gory crap, but she had to keep going because of her contract? And she felt trapped?"

I nodded. "It happens. She wasn't nearly as successful when she first signed on with them years ago. She never told me much about her relationship with them. I was always brought in at the tail end of her writing, before it went to her editor and then after it came back for corrections and needed to go back a second time. Once in a while they asked me to proofread the book at the layout stage because I had a lot of experience with that sort of thing, but even that was tapering off with the last two books. A lot of small presses are letting in-house proofers do that work."

"That sucks for you."

"I'll get by. I just rolled my clients from the traditionally published to the self-published. There's more work than I know what to do with, just with the indies who farm out their work piecemeal."

"Good. Glad to hear it. Not glad to hear that Charlotte may not have been as happy in her work as she could have been, though."

"The writing life isn't as glamorous as most people think. A lot of lonely, late nights and a lot of rejection and hurt feelings. Adding on having to write stuff you're not crazy about would probably depress a lot of folks. Including Charlotte."

Annie tapped her fingers on the stack of papers still on her lap. "I wonder, though. What use would it be to embed something like this in a printout and then leave it in your desk drawer? I mean, wouldn't you want *somebody* to see it?"

"Maybe she was hoping Scott would stumble upon it in the desk drawer... which, come to think of it, is exactly what happened."

"But he probably found it when he did only because Charlotte was already murdered and dead and he was looking for clues. If that hadn't happened, these things might have sat in that desk drawer indefinitely."

"It's also possible that she had those two stories in there for now—because we don't have any idea how long they were there before Scott found them, might have been only a matter of days—but that she had actual plans for them. Maybe she was going to mail them to someone."

"And how exactly was that supposed to work? Look, it took you days to decipher what was going on here... and you were determined. Plus, you're good with details. Someone else might have gotten this crazy thing in the mail and made no sense of it whatsoever. Forever."

"True. Unless Charlotte gave them some sort of hint."

"Seriously?"

"Yeah, okay. You're right. That makes no sense. If you're going to bother to give someone a hint, you might as well just tell them what's going on in the first place."

We sat silently for a few minutes after that. I still wasn't sure what was going on here, but I felt hugely relieved that we had at least punched a hole into the bubble of these manuscripts. We could spend the rest of the afternoon writing out as many of these first letter codes as we could find. I wasn't convinced that every page held secrets like this, but it would be worth our time to sit down together to find out.

I stood up from the couch and turned to go down the hallway to my office.

"I'm going to get us some scrap paper and pens so we can write all these things down. Gather them all up, as many as we can find in both of these stories."

"Great!" Annie exclaimed. I was glad she was here to help. I wasn't sure I wanted to be reading these things all by myself right now. They were a little creepy, especially if they were pleas for help and not just a fun experiment in word play. I reached my office and headed for the desk where I kept a mug full of colored pens.

Grabbing a stack of scrap paper next to the printer, I turned to join Annie at the dining room table.

"Mom? What are you going to tell her husband about all this?" she called from the living room.

"I... I have absolutely no idea," I responded loudly.

"Great. Just great," she said, chuckling. "We're in it now, aren't we?"

Chapter 14

FOR THE REST OF THE WEEKEND, I mulled over the pros and cons of going to Scott and telling him what Annie and I had discovered. All of the pages of that first manuscript had messages running vertically down the left side of the page using the first letter in each line.

New paragraph indents indicated the start of a new word, which made the paragraph lengths even more random and arbitrary than they already would have been. And of course, as I had predicted, now that I knew what to look for, I was flummoxed that I hadn't noticed it at all before Saturday morning's revelation.

We sat down together and spread out the second manuscript later on Saturday afternoon, just before dinner. But that enterprise didn't take long because it was instantly apparent that our little code wasn't working for this manuscript. I got a little testy with Annie a few times when we were trying to make sense of it, and she finally called me on it.

"Mom, it's okay. We don't have to find secrets everywhere."

"I feel I owe it to Charlotte to keep going, though. Until I figure out just what's going on here."

"Mom, did you ever actually *read* this second story?"

"Well, no. Why do you ask?"

"I never read it, either. Maybe it's actually just a story."

I snorted. "Oh, seriously. What are the odds of that?"

Annie swiped the document off the table and righted it so she could look it over. I watched her read for a few minutes.

"So?"

"So," she said, sighing. "I think this is just a story. Which means I don't really want to read any more because it's probably more of the type of stuff of hers that I don't really want to read. At all."

She handed the manuscript out to me, and I immediately grabbed it. "But you're saying it's an actual story? Like, not confusing like the other one?"

Annie nodded. "Definitely. It has a distinct voice to it. I know I don't read Charlotte's books but I'd say this is probably a sort of lost manuscript of some sort."

"Wow!" I said as I thumbed through the second manuscript. We had both become so easily frustrated with the first story that neither one of us had thought to check if the second one read just as badly.

The more I read—bits and pieces as I continued to rifle through the pages—the more I agreed with Annie. This was an unpublished novel. And it definitely had Charlotte's signature writing style.

"Annie, you're right. This has the sound of Charlotte's usual voice. And I can see already that it's an honest-to-goodness story and not some sort of coded printout."

"I wonder if Scott knows about it."

I shook my head. "No, definitely not. When he gave these to me, he assumed they were unpublished stories, both of them. He'd never heard of either of them, he said. He gave them to me precisely so I could proofread them, as I usually do—*did*—for Charlotte before she sent her stuff off to her editor."

"And you're pretty sure this one's not already in print?"

"As sure as I can be, unless she was also publishing under a pen name elsewhere and didn't want me—or anyone else—to know about it."

"Well, that would be rather silly for someone in her position, wouldn't it?"

"Meaning?" I was still flipping through the pages of the "real" manuscript, trying to listen to Annie at the same time.

"Meaning, she already had a reputation for writing some pretty outrageous stuff. Why would she need to hide something she was writing in, what? A more respectable genre? She wouldn't want people to know she was secretly writing literary fiction or something?"

I let a laugh escape. "Ha! Well, I see your point, but there are very good reasons for a writer to assume a different name for a different genre. Stephen King did it for a while earlier in his career. J.K. Rowling has done it. So has Anne Rice."

"Why, though?"

"If they're not ridiculously famous yet, it's sometimes a way to not confuse your readers about which type of book to expect from you. If you're already famous, like J.K. Rowling was, then you might want to let your new story, your new genre speak for itself rather than inviting scrutiny simply because you're already famous. I think Rowling was hoping to see her crime stories garner their own accolades."

"Oh, yeah, that makes so much sense. So, maybe this secret manuscript of Charlotte's is something like that then?"

"I'll see. From looking at it, I don't see any gory scenes jumping out at me, but it would be hard to tell just by flipping back and forth through the pages like this. I have to sit down and read it properly to see what we've got here. And really, that's why Scott gave it to me in the first place. To proofread it."

"What are you going to tell him about the other manuscript? Are you going to tell him about the vertical code?"

I clicked my tongue on the roof of my mouth. "No, not just yet. It's still within the realm of possibility that Scott had something to do with what happened to Charlotte. It's cliché and it's awful to contemplate, but it's also quite possible."

"That's a horrible thought."

"Oh, I know it is."

"They even have a kid, don't they?"

"Yup. A son named Teddy. He's about nine, I think."

"Bad enough he's already lost his mother. It would be really awful if his dad killed her." Annie pulled her feet up onto the couch and wrapped her hands around her pulled-up knees, hugging herself and rocking back and forth.

"Well, I don't want to get ahead of myself one way or the other. If Scott had nothing to do with it, then it'd be even more horrible for him to be accused of it falsely."

"True."

"But since I can't unsay it once I open my mouth about it, I think I'll stay quiet for now and just concentrate on this first story."

"You mean the second story."

"Yes, of course. The first *real* story. I can probably stall Scott on this for a while. He hasn't a clue how long it usually takes me to get through a project, anyway. Plus, he handed it to me without asking if it fit into my schedule. I can take my time and just tell him I'm having trouble finding time amid all my other work."

"Good thinking. But what will stalling gain you?"

"Time. Time to think. Time to figure out what's going on with these hidden messages. Maybe even time to figure out exactly who is to blame for Charlotte's death."

"Oh, Mom, now I can see how you got tangled up in those other murders! You're a natural!"

She was beaming at me. And, as much as I wanted to soak in a little of that rare admiration of one's twenty-something grown child, I also knew I felt awkward about this particular topic. Better for Annie or Seth to admire their mother for her real talents and not because she continued to inadvertently end up in the wrong place at the wrong time. After all, this knack of mine had come at a price more than once, including watching my firstborn languish in a jail cell all night when he was a prime suspect in the last murder I had gotten entangled with. No, far better that I go on to win the Nobel Prize or something. Something worthy of admiration.

"Thanks, Annie, but I didn't really do anything yet."

"You figured out the code."

"It was right there in front of me, though. I'd been staring at that blasted manuscript all week long before you got here, and I hadn't seen what was right there in front of my eyes all that time."

"Don't overthink this, Mom, like you do everything else. You're helping and that's enough. You can at least tell the police about the code, can't you?"

I rubbed a finger under my chin, considering this. "There are good and bad reasons for that, I think."

"What bad thing could come of it? It's not like the Brighton police are corrupt. Or are they?"

She'd moved to the very edge of the seat of the couch. Clearly she now saw this as a sort of live action version of the game of Clue or something.

"Of course they're not corrupt. But if I tell them about this and don't tell Scott first, then two bad things happen. First, the police might be more likely to suspect Scott. After all, I'm sort of a family friend and if I then choose not to share this with Scott, but only with them, then they'll see that I've lost faith in Scott. Second, Scott himself will be upset with me if he's innocent. He'll see exactly why I had gone to the police first—because I thought he could have killed his own wife—and that'll mean I've severed that friendship for good. He'd never forgive me, and I wouldn't blame him."

"See? You are good at this!"

"Whatever do you mean, young lady?" This was quickly becoming frustrating because I enjoyed this sort of sleuthing about as much as I enjoyed a root canal. That is, if I actually had ever had one. Nobody was going to get near my sensitive mouth with razor-sharp metal instruments.

"Look at you! You immediately knew not one, but two reasons why it would be a bad idea to go to the police first. I hadn't thought of either of those until you mentioned them. Bravo, Mom!"

"Yes, yes. Enough of the fangirling, Annie. You have some more episodes of *Gilmore Girls* to binge-watch, and I have an actual novel to read."

"Okay, I get it. Time to go our separate ways."

"Just figuratively speaking, for tonight. I promise I won't look at this tomorrow at all."

"Do you think we can go to the craft fair tomorrow after church?"

"Maybe. It'll be crowded."

"It's always crowded."

"I know. That was kind of my point."

"Geez, Mom. You're such an... introvert."

"You say that like it's a bad thing."

"No comment."

And with that, Annie swiped the remote off the coffee table and curled back up on the couch to binge-watch her way through the entire second season of *Gilmore Girls*. We were both night owls. I'd be up late reading, and she'd be up late watching her favorite TV show of all time. A win-win for us both. I just hoped that Charlotte had indeed switched genres with this second manuscript and that I wasn't about to dive into yet another gory horror story late at night. I had read—and lived—enough of those.

Chapter 15

I T TOOK ME QUITE A BIT LONGER TO DECIDE what to do about what Annie and I had found in that first document, but in the end I decided that my loyalty to my friend Charlotte had to override any misgivings I was harboring about not letting Scott know first. He would just have to have his feelings hurt if he wasn't involved in all of this. And every time I reread the embedded messages we had found, I couldn't help thinking that it was altogether possible— even likely—that Scott had somehow been involved. There wasn't any indication that Charlotte's embedded messages were a joke or were some sort of fun writing game she had devised for herself. She had taken the time to type these things up, format them so that they worked as embedded messages, and then printed them out, only to hide them in her desk drawer for some as yet unknown reason. She wasn't the sort to joke about something like relational issues. And if I could have seen my way clear to believe that these messages were a joke or a game, I would have. But something smelled all too serious here. It didn't read as if it was supposed to be fun.

And that meant that telling someone else about what I had found wasn't going to be fun, either. When Annie went back to college late on Sunday night, I was left alone with our discoveries, and I wasn't altogether happy about what the morning would bring. I didn't want to wait too much longer to tell the police. Time was already ticking, and I'd heard it said that trails went cold if a case remained unsolved too long. No matter who had killed Charlotte, I could not delay alerting the police. This was definitely evidence of *something*, and I would be all too glad to let them sort everything out. I held my opinion of whatever they had done—or not done—in check, reminding myself that I wasn't privy to everything they knew. There could easily be all sorts of good reasons for what looked like a lot of inertia on their part. Guilty or innocent, Scott's opinion and frustration were still just the feelings of one person in this whole mess. He didn't know anything, either, so we would both be wise to be a little more patient with the investigation. And if the knowledge I would bring them could speed things along even just a little, then it would be worth the discomfort I was already feeling about walking into that police station tomorrow morning. I tidied up the stack of papers on the dining room table and set about readying myself for bed. A little light fiction, some herbal tea or decaf coffee. Yes, just the ticket for easing myself off to dreamland. As long as those dreams didn't become nightmares.

"YES, MISS VELAM. What can we do for you?"

Okay, I had introduced myself without fainting. So far, so good, but I was standing there with a stack of papers in my hand—carefully clipped together to prevent any further issues with having to gather them up off the floor—my hand shaking terribly. I probably looked twice as nervous as I felt. I hated the fact that I never was good at hiding my rising panic. Wasn't going to ever have that coveted career as a Hollywood actress at this rate. Probably just as well.

"I... I think I might have some information that you guys might want."

"Might?"

"Sorry. I *do* have information you might want."

"Might?" The officer was smiling at me now. I suppose he meant to put me at ease, but it had the opposite effect on me. I was already feeling off-kilter. His smile made me wonder if they were making fun of me. Not cool, if so. Not cool.

"Sorry again," I amended. "I *do* have information that you *do* want."

He now nodded. "About anything specific?"

Now he *was* toying with me. Or, so it seemed. And I just wasn't in a mood to be toyed with.

I frowned and looked at the papers in my hand, which looked a little steadier than when I had first walked in. "About Charlotte Collins's murder."

That got their attention. The smiling officer took a few steps forward and two other uniformed men stood from their desks. If I had been feeling a little more at ease, I was back to feeling intimidated and frightened.

"What exactly do you have? What sort of information?"

"It'll take some time to explain. Do you have a desk where I can spread out these pages? I need to show you something that came from her house... from her desk drawer."

One of the officers promptly turned to the closest desk and pushed back some papers and a computer keyboard and made room for me. He motioned me over and I took a few unsteady steps toward him.

"Wait just one minute!" said the originally smiling officer, who wasn't smiling anymore. "What do you mean, it came from in her house?"

"I used to be Charlotte's proofreader. I proofread her books."

He nodded. "And?"

Boy, this guy sure knew how to lead a person in a series of short questions. I wasn't sure if I found that helpful.

"And her husband, Scott, invited me and my son to meet with him about a week ago."

"You've met with Mr. Collins?"

I looked from one officer to another, then to the third. They were all kind of staring at me, and I wasn't exactly sure why. I just knew I didn't like it. "Yes. Why do you ask?"

"Just curious. Are you... friends with Mr. Collins?"

"Not particularly."

"Then why would he ask to meet with you?"

"Precisely because I was Charlotte's proofreader."

I was feeling just a tad defensive. I wasn't sure if they were purposely putting me on my guard or whether this was simply how they treated people connected with any sort of major crime. I just knew I had done nothing wrong and needed to make that clear as quickly as possible.

"Why would Scott Collins need to talk to his wife's proofreader once his wife was dead?"

"Because he found some manuscripts in her desk drawer. He wanted me to take a look at them for him."

"What does he expect you to do with them?" asked the officer standing by the cleared desk.

"He expects me to proofread them," I said bluntly. "I kind of thought that was implied." I stood my ground, not moving any closer to the desk until I had a better idea of why they were being so adversarial. Or was I just imagining that? It had started as soon as I had mentioned meeting with Scott. I wasn't imagining their reaction. So, time to tread lightly until I was sure they weren't looking at me funny. Because they were definitely looking at me funny.

"No need to get ornery, miss," said the original officer. I suspected he was in charge, but I had to admit to myself that I mostly thought this because he was clearly the oldest one here. That might not mean anything, but I figured I had to listen to one of these guys more than the others, so Old Smiling Officer won the lottery. Besides, who used the word "ornery" these days? Except cowboys in bad westerns?

"I'm not meaning any disrespect, officer," I said, as calmly and nonconfrontationally as possible. "I just want to share with you what I found in one of the manuscripts Scott gave me."

I walked to the cleared desk and put the manuscript bundle down. The two officers who weren't already there by the desk came over immediately and gathered round. I unclipped the pages, willing my hands to stay steady. I had a feeling that shaking, nervous hands would make me look like I had something to hide. I had no idea how good a judge of character these guys were. Better to take things slow and steady and just get the information in their hands.

I was glad I had made a photocopy of all these pages before I left the house. They were going to want to keep this original once they saw what I had found.

"Scott gave this to me, along with another document about this same length. That one seems to be a straightforward story."

"Written by Mrs. Collins?" asked the younger officer who had cleared the desk.

"Yes, as far as we both know. These were found in her desk drawer at home."

"By Mr. Collins?"

"Yes, that's what he told me at our meeting. That he found them in her office."

All three men nodded. The older man motioned for me to continue.

"This document, though, didn't quite read right."

"Meaning?"

I sighed. This old guy was going to be the death of me with these one-word questions.

"Meaning it was confusing. There didn't seem to be an actual story behind what I was reading. It was odd. Didn't make much sense."

"And you've read other books by Charlotte Collins?"

"All of them," I said quickly. "Every single one. It was my job. And this one wasn't anything like her usual writing. It's not even much like *anybody's* writing, and it's certainly not anything like a good story."

"And this concerns us how?"

I was going to have to make sure this guy never made it onto my Christmas card list. Why couldn't he simply let me go on with my story without interjecting obvious little questions meant to speed me along at a slightly faster pace? His questions only made me stop, think about what he'd just said, and then refocus my next sentence to answer his question instead.

"This concerns you because, after a week of wondering what the heck was going on with this manuscript, I think I finally figured out what Charlotte was doing on these pages."

"Which was?"

I fleetingly wondered what the jail term would be for assaulting an officer right in the police station. Probably not worth finding out.

"Which was embedding separate sentences on each page."

"I have no idea what that means. Can you show us?"

Naturally, that *complete* sentence came from the younger officer next to me on the other side. At least one of these guys could speak in complete sentences like a normal human being. I turned to face him, since he should have been rewarded for his speech patterns with a direct answer.

"Okay, look here..." I spread out the first few pages of the manuscript and pointed to the first letters on each line, letting my finger trace them vertically down the page. "Can you see?"

The young officer leaned over the desk and furrowed his brows as he looked where I was pointing. "What should I be seeing here? I just see random letters here. Should there be... words or something?"

I sighed and tried not to sound exasperated. When I had envisioned how this morning would go, this was about as far from what I had expected as it could get. "Yes, see? There are letters here that spell—" I stopped pointing and stared at the page. "Shit."

"What?" All three officers bent over the page simultaneously. I felt like I was on a sitcom.

"This is the wrong manuscript. I brought the wrong one."

Chapter 16

OW HAD I MANAGED TO MESS UP something this simple? I chalked it up to my nerves at having to go to the police at all, but that didn't make me feel much better. At least, not then when it first happened.

I immediately dashed home in my car and grabbed the correct manuscript, tossing the story manuscript onto the kitchen table and heading back out the door. I felt a moment's guilt as Vlad whimpered at me for going back out the door within thirty seconds of showing up. He probably would have appreciated a short walk in the backyard of the apartment building, but I didn't have time for that.

"I'll be back soon, Vlad," I called as I slipped the door closed behind me again. I could hear him continuing to whine on the other side of the door. I was a bad person. Clearly.

I noted without any surprise at all that every traffic light between my apartment and the police station had suddenly conspired against me as I tried—vainly—to make my way back to the police station with the right stack of papers. At one traffic light, a particularly lengthy one, as I recalled, I shot a glance over to the passenger seat where the stack of papers sat, clipped together carefully with that oversized binder clip. A quick, closer look assured me that I did indeed have the right one this time. Of course I did, but I had suddenly become paranoid about this. The last thing I wanted was to show up at the police station a second time with the wrong papers. The looks they had all given me that first time was an experience I would not soon forget. Any hope I had entertained of this going smoothly had dropped out of the window as soon as I'd told them I had the wrong papers.

Within a span of time that felt way too much like a literal eternity but which was probably more like fifteen minutes, even factoring in traffic in various spots along the way, I was pulling into the very same parking space I had used a half hour before. A strange sense of déjà vu washed over me, but of course this episode had an explanation: I had indeed actually been here shortly before.

"This is very curious indeed," stated the older officer as all three of them bent their heads over the papers I had spread out across the emptied desktop. "I can see why you thought it might be important."

"Because it *is* important, I assume," I responded.

"Possibly," he said, running his finger across one of the pages and skimming down the left-hand column where the letters spelled out one of their cryptic messages. Well, perhaps the messages themselves weren't all that cryptic. It was their purpose, their reason and origin that were most perplexing.

"Why *wouldn't* they be important?" I asked.

"I'm not saying either way. But what I am saying is that, when a horror and gore writer leaves a manuscript behind with an eerie sort of message in it, I'm not going to jump to the conclusion that it's actually a message from beyond, or some sort of cry for help. Things are rarely that black and white."

"I understand. I just don't see this game as something Charlotte would have found any time to fiddle with. It's just not her style."

"But I thought you already told us that you weren't extraordinarily close to Charlotte."

"Not as a friend, no, no more so than two coworkers or colleagues get when they work on projects together for a long time.

But that doesn't mean I didn't know her style as a writer, as someone with limited time and resources. She wouldn't do something like this if it was just for a lark. Just to mess around and have fun."

"Maybe she was trying to develop a brand new story for her readers."

"Well, I read a lot of this 'story' as a story before I discovered what was really going on. And let me tell you, it's not much of a story in that regard. And once you figure out what's going on, then reading just the left-hand line down the side of each page isn't all that entertaining."

"It seems to have caught your attention quite a bit there, lady," he said, and that smug look on his face was enough to make me draw in a long breath as I tried to keep myself from saying something rude—something as rude as he had just said to me.

"That's because I have every reason to suspect it's not just a game, not just for my entertainment. A reader would haven't had that realistic a response. They'd immediately know it was for their enjoyment and not real. And that is precisely what would make the whole experience a lot less fun. The amount of entertainment would be quite minimal compared to reading an entire novel. Readers would feel gypped."

The other two officers nodded in agreement but said nothing, looking to their superior—and elder—for confirmation that they were allowed to agree with me. He nodded eventually, too.

"I see. Yes. Perhaps you have a point there after all."

"I do this sort of thing for a living, you know."

"Waltzing into police stations with stacks of paper?"

I made a slight grunting noise in disagreement. "No, noticing details. Little things that aren't so little."

"Like, bringing the wrong stack of papers into a police station?"

I winced, but he was smiling warmly. I supposed it would be best for me to drop the adversarial undertone and move forward in a spirit of solidarity. He was, after all, just doing his job. And I had wasted their time earlier, so his cheery, light response was perhaps more good grace than I warranted right now, given the circumstances of my first and second appearances today in their station.

"Fair enough. But yes, I've been trying to figure out this manuscript for a week now since Scott gave it to me, and once I saw those messages running down along the left side of the pages, it seemed best to let someone else know. Someone who could perhaps help figure out what happened to Charlotte."

"What was Scott Collins's attitude toward you when he first gave you these manuscripts?"

"What do you mean, exactly?"

"I mean, did he seem like he knew what was hidden in these pages?"

"No, honestly, no. I'm as convinced as I can be that he had no idea what he handed me. He sounded very much like he thought he had only found two of his wife's manuscripts, unpublished stories, and that he thought they might just need to be proofread and passed along to her editor to be published later sometime."

"Do you think he tried to read them?"

"No, absolutely not."

"How can you be so sure?"

"Two reasons. First, he told me he hadn't looked at them much. That he wasn't in a good place to read unfinished stories his wife had written. It was... too soon for that. Second, if he had tried to read this manuscript, he would have immediately noticed what I noticed: that the story wasn't much of a story and didn't read anything like any of his wife's other works. He would have at least thought it was so unpolished that it would never be ready to be published."

"What if he noticed what you noticed... the messages hidden in these first letters of each line?"

"Honestly?"

"Yes, please. We need to work through honesty here or we'll never solve this case."

I squinted at him, wondering if he was being completely honest with *me*. The irony of his statement if he was indeed messing with me for some other purpose was not lost on me.

"Agreed. Honesty and... openness," I said, trying to sound both sincere and yet shrewd. I wasn't sure I had pulled that off, though. He was looking at me as if I had spoken Latin.

"Well, an officer of the law can't always be completely open with folks. You understand that, right, Ms. Velam?" He crossed his arms across his chest and gave me the hint of a frown. I felt like I was being scolded by my dad.

"Why not?"

"This is an *active* investigation. I cannot share everything we know with just anyone. I'm sure you understand my dilemma."

He smiled again, and I returned the smile, even if I felt it a little less than I had a minute ago. "Yes, of course I understand. Still, I'm hoping you can tell me what is going on with Scott. He seems a little shaken by what's happened, and by what he feels is *not* happening in this... *active* investigation."

I thought I might have sounded too standoffish there, but the officer continued to smile at me. "Mr. Collins is supposed to come in here again later this afternoon. We'll catch him up on anything we feel is relevant, and anything we feel at liberty to divulge then. You don't need to worry about Mr. Collins. We'll take care of him."

Now I wasn't sure what to say. How could he have meant that statement? Was Scott really in trouble with the law? Did they suspect him? And since I had just expressed an opinion that sounded as if I was siding with Scott and that I was aware of the police inaction—or, at least, Scott's feelings about it—would they see me in a different light? And how did my bringing this manuscript here change anything, good or bad? I had no idea what they thought about Scott, and they were not divulging that information. But I also realized I had no idea what they really thought about *me*, because they were being careful not to divulge *that*, either. Had I won some of their confidence and respect because I had chosen to come to them with this information? Did they think they could account for my loyalties a little better because of my presence here today?

I was frustrated to find that I couldn't answer any of these questions for myself. And although I suspected the two younger officers were sympathetic toward me and perhaps would have shared some more of what they knew, I also knew that the older officer who was in charge was running the show here and would make sure I was not given any more information than was absolutely necessary to get me to cooperate. And since I also currently had no idea whether they held Scott up as a potential suspect, I was no longer sure how to act around them. Better to find a way to wrap this all up and head out of here. My brain hurt.

"Okay, I see," I said, responding to their statement that Scott was due to come in later this afternoon. "I'll just leave this here then for you, shall I?"

The older officer put his hand protectively over the stack of papers strewn across the desk and smiled widely. "Yes, please do. We'd like to look them over more carefully."

"Not leave any stone unturned," blurted out one of the younger officers on the other side of the desk. The older one gave him a sharp look that clearly said, "Let me handle this." The two other officers seemed to physically shrink back at this look from the older one, and I realized I myself had flinched as his head turned toward them. There was clearly an undercurrent here that I wasn't privy to. And it would be best for me, I realized, if I didn't really acknowledge it too overtly. Better to simply let it simmer underneath and pretend like I hadn't noticed it. Then I could get out of here and onto more familiar ground with people I understood better.

"Gentlemen?"

He turned to me and his visage changed and lightened as if he had not just shot a menacing look at his underlings.

"Yes, Ms. Velam? What can I still do for you?" I watched as he leaned on the desk and tried to look casual.

"Well, I hate to ask this of you three officers, but I do want to at least mention it."

"Yes?"

I wasn't wrong in noticing the overly casual stance as he leaned against the desk. It was definitely fake. He was strung tight as a guitar string about to snap. He was simply practiced at hiding it from folks like me.

"Can you perhaps not show these papers to Scott right away?"

He straightened up and frowned. "Why not?"

"Well, for one thing, he obviously doesn't know I'm here. Or that I'm handing over one of the manuscripts he gave me."

"Oh, of course. No, we can keep that our little secret for now, Ms. Velam." The smile suddenly seemed fake, too.

"Thank you," I replied, thinking privately that this wasn't a little secret. It was a pretty darned *big* secret. If I was right about my findings in this manuscript, this was anything but a little secret.

"Anything else?" None of the three of them moved. They all seemed to freeze in place while they awaited my response. Was there anything else? I couldn't think of anything as important as hiding from Scott the fact that I had been here today. At least until I could figure out some way to tell him what I had done that wouldn't seem as traitorous as it felt. Whether or not they actually told Scott about the manuscript or my presence here today, they were going to eventually use it all against him if they could. Of that much I was increasingly certain. And it felt ugly. And it made *me* feel ugly.

"No, I don't think so," I croaked out before turning my gaze to the floor, where there weren't any judgmental eyes looking at me. Did they find me an ally deep down, or a rat for having given them this information that might implicate someone I called a friend in a murder? It didn't matter what they thought of me now, because I was going to be out of this building as soon as my legs could get me out the door.

"Okay then," said the older officer, now standing clear of the desk with his arms akimbo. "You're free to go." And, of course, he smiled. Again.

I nodded but said nothing more. There wasn't anything else to say. There was, however, a lot to still think and ponder. Mostly, why he would have felt it appropriate to use a phrase like "You're free to go" to someone in my position—someone who wasn't a suspect and who had simply brought them something of her own free will.

I didn't really like this feeling and turned to the front door, with no inclination whatsoever to look back and see if they were still watching me as I left.

Nope, better to just keep moving and get the hell out of here.

Chapter 17

"WHAT I DON'T UNDERSTAND," said Fiona, Brighton Press's head typesetter, "is why they're even bothering to reprint this book in the first place." She held up the previous edition of a dusty theological tome that had seen better days. I took it from her and held it out in front of me as if it were a dead rodent. It certainly smelled like one.

"Um, because it looks like *this*?" I carefully set it back down on the work surface in front of me. Fiona snorted.

"Maybe it looks like this because nobody wants to read it. Did you ever think about that, Maggie?"

I had been kidding, but of course deep down, I had a point. Newer editions of classics came out all the time, and Fiona knew it. She'd been a typesetter for Brighton Press for a lot of years, going back to when everything was coded on ancient computer screens. GUI interfaces had changed her work for the better, and now she was using Adobe InDesign and had more work than she could handle.

"That may be true, but you know you love this work, Fiona. Resurrecting old books is like a pet project of yours. Always has been."

"Books worthy of my time, sure. But this thing is just... so, so *old*."

We both laughed as she gingerly picked up the book off the work table and held it aloft again. She wrinkled up her nose and put it back down.

"Well, at least it'll be appreciative of your efforts, knowing it had no other hopes of new life apart from you."

"Just what I always wanted—a smelly old book in my debt. Yay for me."

"Do I sense a little bit of sarcasm wafting my way, Fiona?"

She laughed and pushed the book aside, to the other side of the table. "I see you're becoming used to my cheery, upbeat ways now that you've worked with me a few times, Maggie."

"I'm quite used to your ways. Now all I have to do is not emulate them."

"My bad then. I didn't mean to drag you down to my level."

"Not a problem. But let's see what we've got here, all right? What have you got ready for me?"

Fiona turned back to her desk and I followed behind her, leaning in to see her monitor after she sat down and called up a folder on her computer. I was hoping she would have at least one full book project for me. I was pretty sure Charlotte's publisher wouldn't be calling on me to proofread any of her final book's layout now that Charlotte wasn't in the picture advocating for the use of her own proofreader. They had their own in-house proofreaders and had only allowed me to tag along because Charlotte insisted. At first they were hesitant, but once she became a big money earner for them, she got virtually anything she wanted. And I turned out to be a relatively minor concession for them since it made their lives easier in the long run.

"I've got a separate nonfiction book that's nearly ready for proofing. I don't think they've assigned that one to anyone else yet."

"I'll take it."

"Don't you want to hear something about it first?"

"Not really," I admitted. "Since I'm losing any future income from Charlotte's books, I'm open to just about any new projects for a while till I can see how her death is going to affect my bottom line."

Fiona continued to scroll around various folders as she spoke. "That's awful. So sorry to hear it. I hadn't really thought of that part of things when I heard what had happened to Charlotte."

"I feel rather... mercenary even stating it like that, but that's part of the fallout for me, at least. And for her publisher, too. It's still a fairly small press, so they're going to feel the pinch of Charlotte's passing."

She shook her head. "It's not terrible to think about it that way. There are bound to be a lot of levels of fallout from this. Not just Charlotte the person, but Charlotte the wife, Charlotte the mother, Charlotte the friend, Charlotte the writer. You're not the only one feeling that side of the loss. Don't feel too guilty about mentioning it. I get it. Really."

"I appreciate it. It's only one client, I know, but she paid well, paid on time, and she was also a friend, so I got to have coffee with her and gab at the beginning and end of every project we worked on together. I'll miss that part, too."

I sighed. This loss was coming in waves. Just when I thought I had wrapped my head around one aspect of it—like Scott and those two manuscripts—another part of the situation hit me. It felt like emotional whack-a-mole.

"Here. This project will be fine for you. Not too heavy, like the Willson stuff. But not completely ridiculous fluff, either. It's a sort of Everyman's theology series. This one's the first to come out, so we'll also be developing a style sheet for it as we go along. Anything you want to add to that along the way, please make special notes of it. Spelling preferences, et cetera. You know the routine."

I nodded. I knew the routine, all right. I enjoyed being the first on a new project that didn't have its own style guide yet. We'd start with the *Chicago Manual of Style* as a base and then work out from there with the specifics that let us deviate from it or add to it. It slowed down a project in the beginning when I was first developing the consistency of styles, but once I got rolling, it was great exercise for the brain to have to juggle around various inconsistencies in the beginning of a project in order to smooth things over and get everything to line up properly. The fact that this was going to be an entire series meant steady work. They'd likely use me as proofreader for each book in the series, if I was the proofreader on the very first book.

"I appreciate this, Fiona."

"Hey, not my call, though I would have chosen you for this project anyway. You're the only one in the stable who can slog through these theological books without tearing your hair out."

I laughed. "Maybe I do tear my hair out but it grows really fast. You never know."

"It must grow *really* fast then. Anyway, thank Alfred for these. I think he's seeing the handwriting on the wall with the newspaper and is trying to branch out into more books, just to cover his ass."

"Handwriting on the wall? Meaning?" I asked,

"You know, Maggie. Newspapers falling by the wayside and all that."

"But the websites keep up, don't they? I've been proofing the online version for years now. In fact, in the past two years, I've done more work for the website edition than the print edition."

"Really?" Fiona asked.

"Sure. It changes all the time, that's why. It's like having a bunch of mini editions going out throughout the day. The print edition is down to just a small morning edition. Not nearly as much work with that these days."

"True. Plus, it's going to go down by four more pages starting in January."

I gasped. "It is?"

"That's what I've heard. Scuttlebutt around the office the past few weeks."

"Well, I suppose I'm not surprised, but I'm not happy about that, either."

"Nobody is, except for the accountants, I think. But it's the way things are headed in this digital age, right? Gotta keep up with the times."

I sighed. She was right. There was no going back to everyone getting the morning edition before breakfast to read during that morning cup of coffee before work. Now everybody wanted to check news sites on their phones on their way to work or at the desk after they got there. The Brighton *Bugle* was only one victim of these changes. The fact that it was a small-town paper meant that it had probably been given a slightly longer life span than a lot of the larger papers. We were still set in our ways—well, some of us were—and we had a respectable number of daily subscribers. But the numbers were falling predictably.

"I can't say that I blame Alfred for adjusting his emphasis then. And to be honest, I prefer the timeline and rhythm of proofreading books more than proofing the newspaper. That fast turnaround can be a bitch sometimes."

"Tell me about it. If we can pick up the slack of the paper with book projects, we'll be fine. It will just be a bumpy transition, I think."

"I'm guessing the reporters and columnists will suffer the most."

"Oh, hell yes. They're already all looking for other gigs to supplement work here. The columnists have had their frequencies cut back in the past six months, as you've probably noticed."

I sighed again. "Geez, this is depressing me. How did we get onto this ugly topic, anyway?"

"Charlotte. You brought up losing work due to Charlotte's death. Your fault. Entirely your fault, young lady." She wagged a finger at me to scold me, and I looked appropriately sheepish and smiled.

"Fair enough. *Mea culpa.* As usual."

"So, other than that, Mrs. Lincoln, how was the play?"

I snorted. "It's been that kind of month, hasn't it?"

"You said it. Now, let's see if I can figure out which of these book files is the most recent so I don't send you the wrong one." She clicked around a few more times, and we were on our way.

I BUNDLED UP MY PURSE AND MY TOTE BAG and turned back to face Fiona. "Hey, thanks for thinking of me with this new series. It'll fit right into the routine nicely right about now." I sighed.

"Any time. You're my favorite freelance proofreader, Maggie."

"Just how many freelance proofreaders do you know?" I asked.

"Including you?"

"Yes, including me."

"Just one."

I smiled. "As I suspected. Thanks for the vote of confidence."

I was turning to leave when I heard a bit of a commotion outside Fiona's office. The door was closed, but I could hear raised voices outside the door, in the main lobby of the *Bugle* offices. Shouting. Not very happy shouting, if I was any judge of voice inflection.

"Are you expecting company?" I asked, clutching the tote bag and purse a little more tightly against my torso and standing still, a little bit back from the door.

"Not really. It's a little late in the afternoon for any of the delivery guys."

"Plus, they probably wouldn't be shouting. Would they?"

"Not unless Ernest ordered another full case of copy paper for the guy to lug in on his own, no."

We both stood silent for a moment, staring at the door but not daring to walk up to it and open it up. Neither one of us was that curious, and I suspected we were also both cowards at heart. At least, I knew I was. It had something to do with self-preservation.

We listened. Now I could hear two distinct voices. One of them was definitely Helga, and she sounded equal parts fury and fear.

I had half a mind to waltz up to that door, open it, and go find out what Helga had gotten herself into. But the other voice was clearly a male—an angry, irate male.

I turned to Fiona. "Should we call someone? Help her out?" Fiona flinched. "I... I don't know."

At that point, the decision was made for us. The door to Fiona's office swung open swiftly, drawing all the way back and hitting the wall hard, bouncing back. It would have closed again had Scott

Collins not stepped forward into the doorway and put out his right arm to block the door's return swing toward him. I felt my heart drop into my shoes but I stood still and said nothing.

Nothing except, "Hi, Scott. Hey... how are ya?"

Add on a stupid, forced little smirk and you'll have a good idea of how I had decided to present myself. Not my finest moment.

"'Hi, Scott'? That's all you have to say to me, Maggie? After—"

He hesitated, but I wasn't sure why. Did he not know what he wanted to say or was he simply overcome with emotion—the bad kind?

"After what?" I asked, immediately regretting engaging him in any sort of conversation. He was a lot madder than anything I'd seen in quite a long time. I glanced around quickly, trying to assess the actual danger levels. Was Scott on the emotional precipice right now, or was he merely generically pissed? I realized I didn't know him nearly well enough to answer that question. Behind him, past the doorway and out in the foyer, I saw Helga standing forlornly, shrugging her shoulders and mouthing "I'm sorry!" over and over. I was pretty sure she couldn't have stopped Scott in his present state of agitation, so I shook my head and tried to shrug back without inflating Scott's ire any further.

"After what? After what you did with the police! That's what!"

"What?" I asked, incredulous and hoping he didn't mean what I feared he meant.

"After taking that manuscript to them before discussing it with me, that's what." He put his hands on his hips and stood there, obviously awaiting my reply. I wasn't sure I had one to give. Well, not one that either one of us really wanted to hear right now.

"I didn't know what else to do with it, Scott! It seemed pretty important that they have that information. As soon as possible."

"So, you needed to tell them so fast that you couldn't even tell me? Couldn't take the five minutes it would have taken to let me know you were going to tell them this big revelation of yours?"

I could tell he was angry, but I truly thought he would simply ignore me and we would no longer be friends. Not that we were very close friends to begin with, of course. So, this scream-fest seemed more intense than I would have guessed.

"Scott, I'm sorry. Seriously. I never meant to hurt you. I just didn't see the relevance of telling you first. That's all."

"How could it not be relevant? You found a friggin' secret message in my wife's manuscript! How could that not be relevant to me, her husband? She's d-dead, for cryin' out loud. Dead. And you might have handed the cops a clue that could tell me just who m-m-murdered my wife, Maggie."

He was clenching his fists so tightly down by his sides that I could see how white his knuckles were from here. I didn't think that was a good sign, overall.

"Scott, calm down. It might mean nothing."

"A secret message in a manuscript? After her website was hacked? And you think it might be nothing? How could it be nothing?"

He stepped forward two full strides and was now way too close to me and Fiona. Fiona wisely stepped backwards and sidled behind her office chair and then the desk itself, but I was still mostly exposed in front of the desk and chair, in direct line of sight with Scott.

I stood still, hoping I didn't look either too much like I was boldly standing my ground or too much like I was a deer in the headlights. Either one might incense Scott still further. I decided to say absolutely nothing, though, so that I wouldn't say something stupid, which I had apparently already done more than once in this conversation.

"Listen, Maggie. My wife adored you and loved working with you. So, for that reason alone, I'll let this go and assume you meant no harm. But let's be clear about one thing right now: This *did* do me harm. More than you probably understand. I found out today that those... *cops...*" He said that last word with enough venom to kill any one of those cops. "...those cops have it in for me. You were right after all."

"I was right about what?" My mind was scrambling to remember any and all prior conversations we had had about the police. But I was also still a bit frightened, so my brain wasn't thinking all that clearly or logically.

"About the police wanting to suspect me of Charlotte's m-m-murder. They suspect me! They do!"

He brought up his fists, unclenched them, and ran his hands through his hair nervously, slapping his own head periodically with both palms as if it might jar something loose in there that he didn't want to think about.

"Scott, Scott! It's all right. Really. I don't think they seriously suspect you."

"Whatever would make you say that? They most certainly do! I just came from there."

"From there... to here? How did you know I would be here?"

"Well, not *just* from there. I went to your apartment first. You weren't there."

My brain was kicking into high gear now. Nobody was at my apartment right now. And I was pretty sure that Vlad hadn't been telling people where I was. So, how did Scott find out?

"How did you know I would be here?"

"I... I just guessed."

"You guessed?" I wondered briefly if this was what it felt like to have a stalker. How would Scott guess something like that? Just randomly guess it?

"I remembered Charlotte telling me that last week before she d-died that you came down here to the paper once a week to check in. I figured it was worth a shot to check here since it's on my way home from your place." He seemed slightly calmer, but that didn't make me feel any better.

I did the mental gymnastics necessary to confirm that yes, if he had been at my apartment and then was heading back to their house, he would indeed come within close striking distance to the *Bugle* office where we now stood. Still, the chances that he would have found me here were slim enough that I felt suitably creeped out. My mind started to list who else knew I was coming here. And my mind came up blank. I had told absolutely no one that I was coming here today because I normally stopped in on Wednesdays and this was only Tuesday.

I again decided to say nothing and let Scott ramble some more, hoping that he would just blurt out something that would put my mind at ease. By this point, it was going to take some pretty big blurting to calm me down and not make me feel like I was in danger.

"Okay, Scott," I said, breaking my own vow to myself moments earlier to say nothing. Apparently I just couldn't wait long enough to have Scott say something randomly. "Okay then, Scott," I repeated, "let's say you coincidentally found me here the one day this week I was going to be here at all, during the one *hour* or so that I was going to be here. Let's say that's entirely possible. Probable, even. Beyond that, why do we need to be talking about this? What makes you think the police actually suspect you of Charlotte's murder?"

He crossed his arms and folded them up against his chest. "Well, for starters, maybe the fact that they started asking me to retell the whole story of where I was that day and what happened. And let's end with the fact that they finally let me leave after, like, three hours, with them saying to me, 'Don't leave town.'"

He was angry again, frowning at me as if it were all my fault. I really hated being the scapegoat here. Had I truly done something wrong? I wasn't even sure anymore.

"Do cops really say that? 'Don't leave town'? I guess I would have thought that was only in the movies."

Scott scuffed a foot along the floor in disgust. Apparently I had said that last bit out loud, when I had only meant to think it in my own little head, safe and sound. "Yes, they really say that, Maggie!" he shouted, and I instinctively stepped backwards, which seemed to trigger his anger still further. Seems I couldn't win any round in this little cold war we were having in Fiona's office. "They really said that *to me*, to be honest with you. And I really don't like that they said that to me."

"I'm... sorry, Scott. Really, I am." And I was. Sorry that he was being implicated. Sorry I hadn't told him what I was planning to do with that manuscript. Sorry that he had to find out about the secret messages that way, inside a police station where it wasn't at all clear what they were thinking about him. It had to have hit him on every emotional level possible. And I had been a party to it, even if it had been mostly inadvertent.

He must have seen the defeated look in my eyes because he didn't lash out at me. I sighed and closed my eyes, taking in a deep breath and trying to think of just the right thing to say. So far, I was batting zero on that front.

"Scott... I'm... sorry."

Well, that was definitely not the most original thing I had ever said, but perhaps my sincerity had shone through after all. Scott sighed and dropped his crossed arms, letting them hang loose at his sides.

"Maggie, I've been through a lot. This isn't helping. But I want to think that one of Charlotte's friends wouldn't deliberately put me in the crosshairs like this. I want to believe that you somehow meant well with what you did."

I wasn't even sure I *had* meant well with what I had done—at least not in the way that he meant. I had known that the police might have turned their sights on Scott. But I had decided—good or bad—to let the chips fall where they may. Informing Scott wouldn't have changed anything if he was innocent. He'd just know a small piece of the puzzle a little sooner. But if he was indeed guilty, then I had been wise to not inform him first. This way, the police could get his unguarded reaction to the news about those secret messages. I hadn't been there to see what his reaction had been, but apparently it hadn't seemed entirely clear to the police that Scott was innocent. I just hoped I hadn't started a misguided witch hunt.

"Scott, listen," I said, taking one tentative step forward as a show of good faith. To my surprise, Scott then stepped backward one step. "I just wanted to move this along as fast as possible. I felt as if I had found out something important when my daughter and I discovered those messages."

"Your daughter?"

"Yes, my daughter, Annie. I asked her to help me read the

manuscripts—to try to figure out what was going on. One of them didn't read right. Didn't read like a story at all. Didn't read like... like... *Charlotte*."

Scott's face fell at this. It wasn't what he expected to hear, and why would he? It made me think that he truly hadn't known anything about those manuscripts. Which, in turn, made me think that he really might not be involved in this whole mess after all. Which, of course, made me feel worse about what I had done by going to the police.

"I didn't realize you had a daughter, Maggie."

"Yes. She's a few years younger than Seth."

Scott nodded but said nothing else. I looked beyond him, out into the foyer, and saw that Helga was still standing out there, as if she was awaiting further instructions from me about how to handle this intrusion. I caught her attention and just shook my head as if to say, "No issue here." She nodded and turned around, heading back to her desk out front. I looked behind me to Fiona, who had, at some point, quietly sat back down at her desk and was fiddling around on her computer. I fleetingly wondered if she was online ready to contact the authorities with a few mouse clicks if things went south here with Scott. She didn't look up. In fact, I was pretty sure she was deliberately avoiding meeting my gaze. I turned back around so as not to draw any more attention to her, in case she really was poised to call in the troops if Scott got out of hand.

"Anyway," I continued, once I started to feel the awkwardness rising again, "as soon as we found out what was going on with that one manuscript, I wrote everything down that we found. Once Annie went back to school, I went to the police, assuming they'd want to know what I had found."

This was all technically true enough, even if I had conveniently left out a lot of my own motives for why I had chosen that specific course of action over other possibilities. If I lucked out, Scott wouldn't ask me that specific question and I wouldn't then have to tell him or be forced into lying, something I really wasn't ready to do just now. Or, ever.

"Can I... can I sit down?" Scott asked, looking around him for a nearby chair. There was another wheeled desk chair to his right, and I pointed to it just as he noticed it and headed that way. I watched as he collapsed into it, suddenly looking completely deflated, almost as if he was a balloon and someone had punched a pin in him. He exhaled loudly and then leaned over, holding his head down with his hands, bent over double, looking like he was trying not to hyper-ventilate. I felt much the same way and looked around for a third chair. Fiona saw me searching and soundlessly pointed to an arm chair sitting up against the wall at the other side of the room. I quietly walked there and dragged the arm chair over closer to Scott. Just as he had done, I collapsed into the chair gratefully, realizing only then how close I was to falling over with all the raw emotion that this situation had brought to the surface. Whether or not we reached some sort of détente here, I was at least going to be seated and wouldn't faint in the process.

"I guess we both needed to sit down," I said, gripping the sides of the chair a little too firmly. I wasn't going to fall off if I gripped it this hard. Scott smiled wanly from his chair a few feet away. I wasn't sure if we would ever be truly friends, but I had a feeling we at least would not end up as enemies.

"Yeah, it's been a long couple of weeks, hasn't it?"

I nodded. I reached across the small gap between our two chairs and patted his hand lightly. "It'll be all right, Scott. It will. Someday. Someday soon." I offered him my best consoling smile, though I wondered if perhaps it didn't look a little too condescending.

"I know. Someday. But yeah, not soon."

Yes, we wouldn't be enemies. I had talked him down off the ledge this time, Maybe we could be friends. Someday. Unless, of course, he *had* murdered his wife.

Chapter 18

WHAT WERE YOU THINKING, GIRLFRIEND?" Helga chided after Scott had left and the tension in the *Bugle* offices had died down a little bit. "That man is guilty as sin!"

"Guilty of what, exactly?" I asked, knowing where she was headed but wanting to make her say it so I could hear her reasoning.

"You know of what. Of killing poor Charlotte." She was tapping her foot in the most scolding fashion, and I had to chuckle whenever she decided to play the mommy role with me. Just because she was about ten years older than I was. Usually she did a good job of inducing the shame and guilt, but this time it wasn't going to work.

"Helga, you don't seriously think Scott killed his own wife, do you?" I tried to sound scolding in response, but I wasn't as good at it, despite having raised two children through their teen years.

"Of course that's what I think, silly goose! And any other sane person would think the very same thing. And, to my mind, it sounds a lot like the police are thinking the same thing themselves."

"*Why?* Just because they told Scott not to leave town? How cheesy is that? Seriously, Helga."

"Don't 'Seriously, Helga' me, young lady. I don't see them telling you or me not to leave town. Just Scott. Just her husband."

"How many Lifetime Channel movies have you been watching this week, Helga?"

"Not nearly enough, apparently. You really need to be careful around that man from now on, Maggie. Promise me."

"Promise you?"

"You heard me, missy! Promise! Now!"

She sounded completely serious, and she probably was, but I also detected a bit of her playful self underneath all the chastising.

"Fine. I promise. But I have a feeling you're wrong."

"Even after finding those secret messages in her writing?"

"Oh, you heard that, did you?"

"Sweetie, everybody in a three-block radius heard that. It'll be all over now. The cat is out of the damned bag, and there is nothing you or I can do about it now."

"Great. Just... great."

I hadn't even stopped to consider that blurting out all that stuff about the secret messages in the manuscript was now going to get talked about all over town. I had to stop and think of who had heard us talking. Me. Scott. Helga. Fiona. And anybody else who had wandered into the main foyer to investigate the loud voices streaming out of the typesetters' room. I could only see Helga standing beyond the doorway, but what she said made me think that there had been others with her at some point. At *that* point. Great. Just great. It was going to be hard enough to keep Helga from blabbing it all over the place. The woman was a gossip magnet, and having her sit out there at the main desk didn't help. She was the go-to person for all sorts of information. Like the general dispensary of all things rumor mill. Usually it was all in good fun, and we had a blast chatting about this or that new employee over the years. But in this case I wasn't comfortable thinking that she might start telling just anybody what she had heard today.

"You know, Helga," I said, hoping to stem the tide of the gossip, "maybe we shouldn't be telling other people about those messages

I found. I mean, I'm not sure they mean anything anyway. Which is why I took them to the police. They have a lot more information about this case than I do, and I assumed they would be able to put the pieces of this puzzle together better than I could."

"Well, we both know that's a load of bull crap, Maggie."

"What is?"

"That the police can do a better job sleuthing than you can."

"Helga, please, not the—"

"You're practically a detective by now, aren't you? This will be, what? Murder investigation number three for you? In the past three years? I think they should give you an honorary badge and gun."

I chuckled nervously. "Yeah, yeah, but those were just flukes."

"Well, sure, you stumbled over dead bodies left and right there for a while. Sure, that part was a fluke. But being there when the shit hit the fan, being there when it all went down. Now that takes some skill. Some mad skills, woman. And you, my friend, have got them."

"Where are you going with this line of thought, Helga?" I closed my eyes and tried not to envision people all over town avoiding Scott because they now thought he had murdered his wife.

"I just don't want you to get hurt, Maggie. That's all. Steer clear of Mr. Collins for a little while. Please?" She leaned in toward me and lightly touched my arm. "Sweetie. Just stay away. For now."

"No problem, Helga. There isn't anything I really need to say to Scott right now."

"But don't you have that other manuscript of his? Of Charlotte's? I thought he asked you to look them both over."

"Yeah. What's your point?"

"My point, Maggie, is that you'll have to contact him about that one at some point, won't you? If it's a real novel? One he might want to see published someday?"

"Well, yes, but—"

"But nothing, sweets. Stay away. He doesn't need to hear from you until we're sure the police have cleared him."

"I thought you said the police weren't interested, weren't going to solve this thing."

"You know what I mean,"

"I'm afraid that I don't, Helga. I'm a little confused right now."

"If the police let him go and start to focus on someone else, then go right ahead and work with Scott. Until then, lay low. Don't touch that manuscript. There's no hurry, is there?"

"No, not really. And I'm not entirely convinced that the cops think Scott did anything wrong."

"'Don't leave town, Scott.'" She said this in a low, menacing voice. She sounded like a cartoon character. Come to think of it, she usually sounded like a cartoon character. I loved this woman. This crazy, mothering, smothering woman.

"Okay, I get your point. I'll stay away."

"Now that we have all that settled. What else is new with you, chickie?" The frowny face immediately disappeared—now that she had secured my obedience—and she was beaming like her usual cheery self.

"Not a thing, Helga. Not a blessed thing."

BACK AT MY DESK LATER THAT DAY, I got curious about what was going on with Charlotte's case. I found myself clicking on the bookmark for her website, hoping to see something new. But it was the same as the last time I had clicked there. I hit refresh just to be sure I wasn't seeing a cached copy of the site, but nothing changed. The cryptic "SOMEONE WILL DIE!" line was mercifully still gone, so I assumed Seth had not changed anything else behind the scenes with her blog site. I stared at the screen for a while before clicking on the News tab. There was now a relatively generic, harmless statement from Charlotte's publisher about her death, saying very little about its cause. Just mentioning that she had died suddenly and unexpectedly (well, after all, who expects to wake up one day and get shot, right?). No other added information and certainly no hint that the police were involved and investigating a murder. That was probably best. You can't unsay something, after all, Still,

I suspected that Charlotte's readers wouldn't be satisfied with this general statement that was *so* general as to be offensive to anybody who read the news.

And that gave me an idea. I Googled Charlotte's name just for fun. Of course, I immediately found out that it wasn't actually fun at all. The entire first two pages of results were various social media and news sites articles about Charlotte's murder. Every low, slimy site and outlet was weighing in with their own conspiracy theories and ideas on what had actually happened to Charlotte, and it was disconcerting to see just how many of them leaned toward Helga's anti-Scott stance. I consoled myself that many of these sites were only using the default "the husband did it" theory and hoping to win readers and clickers. The clickbait nature of half of these search results was strangely comforting and dismaying at the same time. I wasn't sure how that was possible, but it probably had something to do with my own underlying ambivalence.

Although I had decided that Scott wasn't the culprit, Helga had a point about steering clear at least until I could ascertain what was really going on. And it wasn't like Scott had an airtight alibi or a complete lack of motive. All marriages had their dirty, seedy underbellies. All of them. Whether or not either partner could handle it was a different matter entirely. What if Scott couldn't handle his wife's fame? Or, more particularly, her fame in a rather seedy genre?

I shook my head clear of all this rumination, for now. Back to the matter at hand. The website. Looking for all the world like an inviting, normal website. My Google results hadn't turned up anything yet about the "SOMEONE WILL DIE!" line on the website. We weren't entirely sure how long it had been actively visible on the site. Maybe very few people saw it.

On a whim, I picked up the phone and called Seth, who picked up his phone on the second ring.

"Mom?"

"Hey, Seth, I've got a question for you."

"Homemade chicken noodle soup."

I balked. "What?"

"Homemade chicken noodle soup!"

"What the heck are you talking about?"

"The answer to your question." I could hear the humor in his voice.

"And just what question did you think I was going to ask you?"

"What I want for dinner tonight when I come over. Of course."

"Oh, nice. That was subtle. Fridge empty again?"

"Not if you can count two beers, some parmesan cheese, and a mysterious Chinese food container."

"Yeah, that's pretty empty. You wanna come over for dinner?"

"Sure! Thanks! Now, what was your real question?"

I chortled. "My real question was whether you can tell how many hits a website gets on any given week... or day."

"Sure. I assume you mean Charlotte's website here, yes?"

I could hear clicking in the background, plus some sort of vague roaring and other unidentifiable noises and ambient sounds. "Yeah. What's that... what's that noise?"

"What noise?" *Click.. click... click... roarrrrrr...*

"Is that Skyrim?"

"Ha. Yeah. Skyrim."

"Mm-hmm."

"Yeah, I have a visitor counter on her website. She asked me for one at the beginning. Actually, I guess it was her publisher who asked her to keep track, so we added a counter right away. Been there the whole time."

"Can you access it? Does it break down visitors by day, do you think?"

"Yeah, it tracks day by day, unique visitors, repeat visitors."

"How does it tell a unique visitor from a repeat visitor?"

"IP addresses."

"You're going to start speaking *that language* again soon, aren't you?"

"That language?"

"You know what I mean. That language you speak when—"

"Oh, *that* language!"

"Yes, that one."

"Yeah, I'm gonna start speaking it. But I'll let you off the hook a little bit, okay?"

"Good."

"Let's just say that yes, I can tell with that counter how many people visited Charlotte's website on any given day. Now, why do you want to know something like that? And what particular day are we talking about? A random date or something specific?"

"Something specific. Very specific. Like, that day we discovered the 'SOMEONE WILL DIE!' thing on there. That day."

"Do you remember what that date was?"

"It was what? Two days before she was murdered?"

"I thought it was about three days, actually."

"I can find out the exact date. I just wanted to know if it was possible. It's good to know that it is."

"Why do you want to know?"

"I was Googling Charlotte's name and—"

"That's never a good idea, Mom."

I burst out laughing. "You know me too well sometimes, Seth."

"And while you were Googling Charlotte's name, what horrible stuff did you come across? Tell me that."

"Well, the strange thing was, I came across a lot of news sites and social media posts about her death, you know?"

"I would have expected that. But I have a funny feeling that's not why you're calling and asking me if we can track the visitors to her website. I've been to her website this week. I've seen that boring statement from her publisher. That's not going to attract too many people to her site, now, is it? They're probably all flocking to the sensationalistic articles on those other sites. The ones with murder suspect theories. The ones discussing whodunnit."

"You know, you're sounding mighty cynical for someone so young."

I heard him laugh from the other end of the phone. I also still heard the mouse clicks and roaring coming from the game on his ridiculously oversized computer screen. Those geek types really knew how to set up a desk for work and gaming.

"I'm not cynical. Not really. I'm just curious about what you want that information for. I can't think of a reason offhand, but I know you have one. That brain of yours is always in high gear."

"Well, I was wondering why none of my Google search results were turning up articles about that 'SOMEONE WILL DIE!' bit on her website. I wouldn't have worried about it, generally speaking. It wasn't a major hack and it didn't steal anybody's identity."

"That we know of."

"Seriously? Could it have stolen someone's identity?"

He laughed again, louder this time. "No, of course not! Just messing with you!"

"Now that's just mean." More laughter. "Anyway, once she was found dead, I would have thought anybody who saw that little hack thing would have started talking about it. Somewhere. Anywhere. We did see it, right? I'm not just making that up in my head, am I?"

"No, we both saw it, Mom. It was real. And it was live on her site. Don't add on hallucinations on top of everything else, all right?"

"Okay. Anyway, I'm curious to know just how many people might have visited her site that day. If it was only a small handful, then that would at least explain why there aren't any search results about it."

"And what if there are a lot of hits on that day?"

"Well, then we start some conspiracy theories of our own, I guess."

"Plus, are we even sure that this was only up on that one day? Sure, it was up the day we saw it, but it could have been up for hours before that, right? Days, even?"

"Well, I don't know."

"When was the last time you'd visited her site before that day?"

I didn't have to think very long. "Not for a while. It wasn't something I had to visit often. She didn't change it much except when a new book came out."

"So it could have been up for days then."

"Probably not. I mean, I'm sure Charlotte visited her own site every day, right? Wouldn't an author visit her own site every day? And she didn't say anything until that day with us."

"If the site doesn't change much then she might not visit it every day, no. Too bad we can't just ask her directly."

I sighed. He was right. I now wished we had finished dealing with this strange issue before Charlotte had died. It was going to be a lot harder to find out how long this hack had been actively on the site without being able to talk to Charlotte herself.

"Maybe Scott would know. Maybe Scott visited her site more often and knew."

"Touchy subject right now, Seth. Plus, wouldn't he have told us if he'd seen it before we did? I mean, something like that? It was scary at the time, even before what... what happened to Charlotte."

"Well, but what if... well, no, never mind. I didn't say anything."

"What, Seth? Say it. Just say it. What if *what*?"

"If Scott was the one who... you know. Who killed her. Then he might not have said anything beforehand. Might not want to draw attention to... what he was planning to do."

"You have one sick, twisted mind, my son," I said, and although we both laughed a little, I felt an undercurrent of truth in what he said. And, it wasn't pleasant at all.

Chapter 19

WE HAD A BIT OF A VERBAL TUSSLE about which of us was going to contact Scott about the website. I wanted to do it myself, but Seth said it would be a lot better for both of us if he was the one to call Scott. After all, he was still in Scott's good graces—assuming Scott wasn't into guilt by association too much—and he was the resident IT tech geek in this little ménage à trois. I thought better of always wanting to be the one in control and let Seth do the talking this time.

As per Seth's request I made the homemade chicken noodle soup for dinner. And as per Seth's usual M.O., he arrived early, not wanting to risk missing out on a free home-cooked meal, even if it was only soup, salad, and good crusty bread.

"How did it go?" I asked as we were sitting down at the table. I had everything ready for him and had the entire table set, knowing he would walk in the door already hungry. And, as I had anticipated, he dived right in, grabbed the soup spoon, and ladled up several mouthfuls in rapid succession. I found it charming that my mom's heart never got tired of seeing one of her children enjoying her cooking. Especially when said mom wasn't even all that great a cook to begin with. Sometimes it was all about the simple things, or just about the fact that Seth was pretty lazy. His idea of cooking was heating up the ramen noodles in the microwave. I had tried to convince him that most of what he thought of as Mom's home cooking was really pretty easy to make, precisely because I hated cooking almost as much as he did and had learned a bunch of shortcuts to make that unpleasant daily task a little easier for myself.

Still, it was easier to head over to Mom's house and sample some of hers instead. Easier and cheaper.

"How did what go?" he asked, his single-minded focus on the bowl of soup in front of him undiminished by my question.

"The phone call."

"What phone call?"

Okay, now he was crossing a line. I wasn't sure if he was really so set on the soup that he'd forgotten why he was here, or if he was messing with me. With Seth, it was hard to tell the difference.

"Seth. The phone call. To Scott. Remember?"

"Oh yeah, that." He slurped two more spoonfuls of soup into his gullet before answering. Nothing like adding a little suspense to my already stressful day, week, month.

"Yes, dear son of mine. That."

He laughed and nearly dribbled soup down the front of his ragged old sweatshirt. I smiled at him, glad to see I could still find a way to get his goat.

"Well, not much happened. At least I don't think so. We talked for a while, and I kind of got the impression that he doesn't know much about Charlotte's website at all."

"Oh," I said, a little discouraged at this news. "Seems odd that both he and Charlotte were so terrible at maintaining any sort of online presence, don't you think?"

"Mom, a lot of people know how to check Facebook on their phones, but don't have the first clue how to set up or update their own blog or website. That's not all that unusual, really."

"I guess," I conceded. I knew how to keep my own site up to date, but then again, I'd given birth to a geek, so I had a distinct and huge advantage over most people in that regard.

"Besides, I half expected that to be the case."

"Why?" I was now also wolfing the soup down. It had turned out particularly good this time, and I was enjoying the aroma of the chicken broth on this chilly day.

"If Scott could maintain a website, they wouldn't have been paying *me* to help her do it, right?"

Sometimes those obvious things stared me right in the face. Apparently my attention to detail didn't extend to bits of logic and external reasoning.

"Oh, yeah. Now that seems obvious, doesn't it?"

He slurped some more and went back to paying more attention to his soup than to the woman who gave birth to him. I didn't take it personally. I was quite used to it after all these years.

"So where do we go from here?" I asked, though I suspected I was thinking out loud and not really engaging Seth in anything like a serious discussion anymore. "I don't know where things go from here."

"Mom, you're talking to yourself again."

"I thought I was talking to you, but apparently not."

"What?"

"Nothing. I was just wondering out loud about how to handle Scott at this point."

"Well, at least I didn't really lose a *huge* client over all this," he said. "I mean, it was easy work since she didn't want anything fancy. I just had to set things up and then let it go."

"And help her when she had problems working in the blog dashboard, too, right?"

"What do you mean?" He'd gotten really good at having this conversation while still maximizing the amount, of soup, bread, and salad he managed to get into his stomach. It had to be a twentysomething guy thing because I knew I wasn't very good at it. By now I would have either lost my train of thought or slobbered soup all over myself. Or both.

"She was constantly telling me how she couldn't even manage

to get anything done on the site. Couldn't update her blog, couldn't ever remember her password, even. I was beginning to wonder how she ever got any of her books written. She made herself sound like a complete moron about the computer. Or, the online world, at least."

I shook my head, remembering so many conversations with her in which she had a blank look on her face. The woman was completely clueless about most of the internet. I should have been surprised that she wasn't writing historical fiction set in some faraway place hundreds of years ago. That sometimes seemed about as technologically savvy as she could get. But perhaps I was being a little snarky, having been online myself since the earlier days before Windows was a thing. My first computer hadn't even had a mouse, or a hard drive.

"What?" I said, having caught just the tail end of something Seth had been saying. I had completely zoned out and missed it... and I wasn't even the one trying to eat and talk at the same time anymore.

"I said, that doesn't seem to jive with my own dealings with her. Sure, she needed help in the beginning, and even tried to make it sound like she could barely find her way around a keyboard. Which is crazy. She really didn't call me for help very much, and even when she did, it wasn't all that serious and she picked up on what I was saying kinda fast."

I nodded. I wasn't sure what to do with this information, but I nodded just the same.

"Of course, though," he continued, stopping briefly to ponder something, the soup spoon poised in midair above the bowl. "Well, I mean, she started calling me a lot in the past few weeks."

"What do you mean, calling you a lot?"

"Like a couple of times a week. Before that, she really wasn't calling me more than once a month or so."

"Wow. What changed? Do you know?" *Now* he had my attention. It seemed weird that the woman who continually whined to me about her lack of online skills wasn't calling Seth all that much up until a few weeks ago. I had the impression, based on things she had been telling me, that she needed his help every couple of days.

So, why hadn't she needed his help all that much before this recent change in behavior? Something wasn't adding up.

"Haven't got a clue, no. But suddenly her site was really, well, glitchy. That's the best word I can think of to describe it."

"Glitchy?" He might have thought it was a great word, but I certainly didn't. I still didn't know what that meant about her change in behavior.

"Yeah, glitchy. I'd go to her house, and she'd try to explain to me what had happened. I'd ask her what she had been doing just before, and she almost never had a good, clear answer. It was like everything I had shown her, everything I had taught her, was gone. Whoosh, right out of her brain," he said, whipping one hand over his head and back. I was glad it wasn't the hand with the soup spoon in it, or I would have had a lovely wet streak of soup broth across the dining room ceiling.

"Well," I said, "I knew she didn't like learning much about how the online world worked, at least not behind the scenes."

"I could see when I checked the site—which I do every week as a part of my checks of all the sites I help out with—that she was updating her blog and getting new information on new books on there just fine. So what gives? What changed?"

"Yeah," I said, breaking off a crust of bread from the heel on the plate sitting between us. "Exactly. What changed?"

"And," he continued, grabbing that last piece of bread before I got a hold of it—he knew me too well. "And, why now? I gotta think it's no coincidence that this happened only a few weeks before she died."

"Meaning what?" I asked through a mouthful of bread crust. It was really good, crusty bread, but it certainly made talking a wee bit difficult.

"Meaning she goes months and months—*and months!*—without calling me and then all of a sudden she needs help with every little thing? That just seems weird to me."

"And to me," I agreed. "But if it's not a coincidence of timing, then what are you saying, exactly? That her murderer somehow has something to do with the timing?"

"Well, I don't know. That seems really weird then, doesn't it? And it makes no sense. If she was afraid of something, or someone, why would she start calling me to get me to believe she suddenly needed help with her website? If someone wanted to put out a cry for help, there are a gazillion better ways to do that than to start asking me, of all people, for help with her website."

He shrugged and dipped his soup spoon back into the bowl. He had said his piece, given his opinion, and now the soup had regained the top slot of importance.

"That does seems odd," I agreed. I would have to think this over. Why on earth would whoever killed her do something that then made Charlotte start asking for unnecessary advice from Seth? I didn't buy the possibility that she had completely forgotten everything and needed Seth to come back and re-teach it to her. And Seth was right that a cry for help could have come through easier and more helpful channels than through her webmaster. Especially since it didn't sound as if she actually put out any sort of real cry for help. She just started asking him for the same old advice on how to update her site, her blog. That hardly seemed like the kind of thing that would have garnered much attention from Seth. Nothing there to make him alert the authorities, or alert *anybody*. It just would have seemed like she was ditzy and forgetful, and Seth definitely had plenty of clients like that. For some folks, instructions on how to do things on a computer just didn't compute. I hadn't thought Charlotte was one of those people, but it wasn't completely outside the realm of possibility. Besides, just who would she feel she needed to warn Seth about by having him come over to the house?

"Hey, Seth," I said, leaning across the table. That got his attention.

"Yeah?" The soup spoon hovered, but only for a few seconds, then it found its way into his mouth and he slurped more of the soup.

"She had you come over to her house during these recent... well, lapses in computer memory. Right?"

"Yeah. Why?"

"I mean, these weren't phone calls or emails, right?"

"Well, she'd start by emailing me, trying to explain the problem, but she really couldn't express herself very well, so I'd end up suggesting that I just come over so she could show me in person on her computer. Getting her to figure out how to take a screenshot would have taken more time and been more frustrating than me just getting in the car and driving over to her house to take a look."

"She couldn't express herself very well?"

"Yeah, why? Is that weird?"

"For a writer? For a *best-selling* writer?"

He stopped, the spoon again in midair over the bowl. "Oh. That never even occurred to me. I have so many clients who just don't speak the language, so to speak. I didn't even stop to think that a writer would at least be able to communicate the *problem* somewhat better than the average clueless computer user."

I shook my head. Something wasn't adding up here. Even when Charlotte was trying to sound as if she couldn't update her own website, she still at least understood the situation well enough to be able to talk about it, to write about it. She was a good communicator. Even if she had needed Seth to come over to fix something, she would have been able to at least give him a decent idea of exactly what was wrong. Had she suddenly gotten terrible at everything in those final days? I hardly believed it. She seemed fine to me in every other respect.

"What are you thinking here, Mom?"

"Don't know. I just know that someone is hiding something from someone else."

"Well, it's not me, that's for sure."

"No, of course not. Not you, And not me. I hate to even ask this, but was Scott ever home during the times you went over there to help Charlotte?"

"You mean the times recently?"

"In those last few days or weeks. After things changed and she started contacting you again to come help her."

"Let me think...."

I was feeling weird about asking this and wasn't even sure which answer I preferred.

"No, I don't think so. I don't remember running into him at the house while I was there, anyway. And they have that single-story ranch house, so it would have been pretty easy to tell if someone else was in the house with her."

Now I was stumped. "So, why? Why get you over there? Obviously not to protect her from someone else who was in the house."

"Unless he left sometime in the interim while she was waiting for me to show up. Maybe just knowing another person was coming over would have made him leave." He shrugged.

"No, not if he killed her. At least I don't think so. He'd want to stick around to see if she spilled the beans, or if she tried to tell you she was scared of him or something. Right?"

He shrugged again. "Sounds right to me, but what do I know? What does either one of us know? It's not like we know anything about how the mind of a murderer works, right?"

"I sure hope you don't know, Seth. Otherwise, no soup for you!"

He laughed and almost spit soup out of his mouth. "See, I wouldn't risk a complete soup boycott. No, I don't have a clue how a murderer thinks. And I like it that way."

"Something just doesn't make sense here, and I'm bound and determined to get to the bottom of it. For Charlotte's sake."

Seth shrugged and bent his head to his dinner one more time. "Of course you are."

I was starting to think I had a reputation for this sort of thing now.

Chapter 20

CONTINUED TO FRET OVER WHY CHARLOTTE would put on a
farce about being completely incompetent with computers. This
felt like something really important to the investigation, and yet
I also felt as if I should keep it to myself for now. Although Seth
was in on it because we had discussed it at dinner the other night, I
didn't engage him further in conversation about it. For now.

This new wrinkle, coupled with the strange embedded notes in
those manuscripts from Charlotte, had my brain working overtime
and I wasn't going to be able to fully concentrate on my work until I
had found a way to put the pieces of this puzzle together and make
them fit. I was worried that I was trying to fit a round peg in a
square hole (to continue but revamp some metaphors).

Just because these two things had happened—one of which
seemed far more concrete than the other—didn't necessarily mean
they were tied together. After all, there were *tons* of things I knew
about Charlotte. She liked to drink her coffee black. She disliked
pastries with her coffee. She had a secret dream to color her hair
purple, at least on one side. Those were part of who Charlotte was,
just like her supposed lack of computer skills. That didn't mean I

had to start searching for a deeper reason why she disliked pastries. Somewhere in all this mess there was a line that clearly delineated which facts about her would aid me in my own queries and which were just random facts about her that had no bearing on her murder. I had to remember to keep my big mouth shut about some of these things so I didn't lead myself—or, worse, the police—down the wrong path. I wasn't vain enough to assume that the police were necessarily listening to anything I had to say about Charlotte's murder, but I also didn't want to look as if I were leading them astray, on purpose or even accidentally.

So, on that particular morning, I sat at my desk, using the mouse on my desktop computer to scribble all over the PDF layout of a book I was proofreading for an indie author. I tried to keep my mind on my work, but it became increasingly difficult to focus on things like punctuation and font sizes when my brain only wanted to zoom in on Charlotte's state of mind in her final days. If that website hack or intrusion or whatever it was hadn't started up again, and if that "SOMEONE WILL DIE!" wasn't a fluke—and I was pretty sure it was no fluke—then it had an origin, a genesis with someone, somewhere. Sure, there was an off chance that it was just your typical troll or hacker who does these sorts of things to get his jollies. But the timing of this one, coupled with the fact that it had said someone would die, kept me coming back to it as a clue. Or, at least, as a starting point.

Most people who murdered a single person had a reason. Usually what *they* considered to be a very good reason. And they really didn't want to tip anyone off that they were about to kill someone. Most importantly, they didn't want the upcoming victim to see it coming. So, why would someone throw out into the universe this hint, this massive warning, only days before killing Charlotte? At the time neither Charlotte nor I—nor Seth, now that I thought about it—took the message as a true death threat. It looked like a typical troll trying to get some attention. I knew Seth saw so much trolling that he likely hadn't thought twice about it at the time, except that we needed to get rid of it, for several reasons. Seth wasn't entirely sure it was harmless, so that was his primary concern in getting rid of it. There was also the added issue of it being ugly and scary. Initially, Charlotte might have thought it could provide its own sort of odd publicity if it didn't do any damage otherwise: it could be a sensationalistic story that would ramp up book sales if it brought people to the site to see the flashing warning for themselves. But she had pleaded with us to get rid of it and worried that too many fans had already seen it. I thought of that old adage that even bad publicity is good publicity. In Charlotte's case, of course, with that eerie genre in which she wrote, having a spooky message pop up on her website wasn't the worst thing that could have happened to it. Still, she had seemed relieved when Seth got it off her site so quickly. But until I talked to Seth, I wouldn't know just how many people had seen it.

"So you're saying it was in the hundreds then?" I asked him when I took a work break and called him on the phone.

"In the high hundreds. Up near a thousand people."

"And those are different people, for sure?"

"Well, different IP addresses, anyway. That's probably pretty close to the right number of unique people, though. Some people might check Charlotte's site through different devices—a tablet, a phone maybe, or an actual computer—but I'd wager that most people who check out Charlotte's site do that only once a day anyway. So, let's just say it was nearly a thousand visitors to her website that day when the warning message showed up."

"Thanks, Seth. That's helpful, and yet, not."

"How is it not helpful?"

"Well, don't get me wrong. I needed the information, so I'm glad that now I have it. But that number is a lot higher than I would have hoped. It doesn't give me any information I can really use."

"You're still trying to figure this all out, aren't you?"

I played dumb. I was pretty sure it wouldn't work, but I tried.

"What do you mean, figure this all out?"

"Mom. You know. You're doing it again. Maybe you should stop."

I sighed. "So sue me. Charlotte was my friend as well as a client. And she was young and talented and had a lot to offer to the world. Is it wrong to want her to have some justice?"

"No, of course not," he conceded. "I get it. I just don't want to see you get into trouble. Like last time."

"Seth, honestly..."

"Or the time before that."

"What's your point?"

He snorted. "Geez, Mom, I love when you decide to play dumb. You're not nearly as good at it as you hope. Just be careful. Okay?"

Sometimes I got tired of my kids and my friends all telling me to be careful all the time. Had I suddenly become clumsy, or did I now have a knack for collecting situations that required a little more sleuthing than the local authorities were able to do? That might be the unanswered question of the ages for me. For now, though, I had to file this new bit of information about the number of website visitors away because it wasn't going to easily point me toward the guilty party. If only a few people had seen this, I might have found a way to contact them online. But I wasn't about to contact nearly a thousand people about this. I would have to sit down with Seth to see if he could help me find out who had been on Charlotte's site tinkering around with her dashboard and uploading that creepy message that day. I tried not to think too much about whether the police were pursuing this same angle. It seemed important to *me*, but if they weren't following up on this lead, then what did that say about how important it truly was?

For now I had to do something to move forward. This freelance project was going to have to sit a little while longer. And that was all right. The deadline was still a few weeks away, and it seemed like a fairly straightforward project so far. Taking the rest of the day off today to do a little more sleuthing wasn't going to set me back all that much. So, I closed down the PDF after saving my work and turned off the light in my office. It was time. Time to contact first Scott, and then Seth. And sure, I was going to be careful. But since I didn't currently think Scott was guilty of murdering his wife, I wasn't going to go to ridiculous lengths to be as careful as Helga would have wanted me to be.

Chapter 21

I WAS SURE THAT SCOTT SENSED that I had no ill will toward him and just wanted the same thing he wanted: an end to this madness and Charlotte's killer behind bars. If that killer was Scott after all, well, then I had a problem. But I'd have to jump off that bridge when I came to it, and not before. There had to be something about that innocent-till-proven-guilty bit, right? If it didn't apply in a situation like this, then exactly where DID it apply? Scott was going to get my goodwill until I was sure he no longer deserved it. And I tried to not think about the fact that the authorities literally had no one else lined up as a possible suspect. That was a sticky point I'd have to address later.

The first order of business, though, was to sit down with that second manuscript and read it more carefully. If this was indeed an actual story and not another cryptic puzzle from Charlotte beyond the grave, then I should do it justice and sit on the couch with it—and a cup of hot coffee—and pay better attention to what I was reading: as a story this time and not as some eerie encrypted message. As a reader this time and not as a proofreader or amateur sleuth.

By the time I was a third of the way through this second manuscript, though, I had been moved to tears twice. The prose was elegant and stirring. The characters were realistic and believable. The dialogue felt natural and paced the story smoothly. I wanted to drop everything else in my life and stay up for as long as it took to read the entire thing.

This was hardly the typical sort of Charlotte Collins story I had grown accustomed to reading as her proofreader. Where was the gore? When would the bondage-lite stuff come in? So far it was nowhere in sight... and I was loving every minute of it. I had to remind myself that Charlotte really could write well, and that she was perfectly capable of turning out beautiful fiction like I was reading right now. So, I thought, why wasn't she ever doing that? Why hadn't she given up on the horror and dark fantasy stuff if she knew she could write like this?

Because Charlotte was dead—and murdered, at that—then that question might turn out to be a question for the ages, I thought, as I let myself fall into the final beautiful, fictional world of Charlotte Collins—a place I never wanted to leave.

AFTER A FEW HOURS, I had come to the end of the printed manuscript in my lap. The story itself wasn't over—apparently Charlotte had died before she could finish it—but it had drawn me in so completely that I had to reacquaint myself with real life around me for a moment, to remember where I was and when I was. I needed to contact Scott Collins to let him know that this second printout was something altogether different from that first one. He deserved to know certain things about his wife's talent—things that might never come to him through ordinary means. And, as far as Scott, Seth, or I knew, I held the only copy of this beautiful fragment of Charlotte's imagination. Much as I would miss it, I also knew I had to give it back to Scott. And soon.

But I wasn't entirely sure Scott would talk to me about something as innocuous as the *weather*, let alone about his wife's murder. He had technically forgiven me for blabbing to the police about the first mystery document with the words embedded down the left edge, but I had a feeling he was still a bit pissed that I had mentioned it to them in the first place. The head didn't always work in alignment with the heart, after all. I had to find a way to talk to him about this second manuscript and how vastly different it was from that first one.

I had a hunch Scott's first reaction to me would be to keep me at arm's length, but if I could push him, nudge him a little bit, he would relent and let me bring the manuscript over to discuss it. At the very least, he would be curious to see and read it himself. And if I could communicate my feelings of amazement at this new style of writing from his now-departed wife, he would definitely want to have it back.

While I debated various ways of starting a phone conversation with Scott in which I would ask to bring the manuscript back over to talk about what I had discovered, I took that lone copy back to my office and put it into the document feeder of my printer. After checking the paper drawer to make sure there was enough blank paper there and then hitting the Copy button, I padded back out of the office toward the kitchen, listening to the machine as it whirred softly, making a copy of Charlotte's final written work. I had already copied that first document, with the cryptic messages in it, before I had handed it over to the police. Seemed like a proofreader's habit to simply make copies of projects and documents before going any further.

As I poured myself another cup of hot java and opened the fridge to reach for the creamer, my cell phone chimed the notification sound for a new text message. I had left the phone on the coffee table last night, unplugged, so I would have to remember to charge it back up before I next headed out of the house. Coffee in one hand, I strode to the living room and swiped the phone off the low table, sinking into the sofa and sipping some coffee before putting the mug on a coaster on the coffee table.

One swipe and the text message was open. It was from Seth.

dont contact scott. he just called 2 chew me out.

Well, I wasn't going to let that text go without pursuing it further. I had no idea what Scott would have needed to scold Seth about at this stage, but I was certainly going to find out. I tapped on Seth's name and his contact profile came up. I touched the small green phone icon and heard the phone ring once… twice…

"Mom?"

"Seth, what happened? Are you okay?"

"Sure, I'm fine. Didn't mean to worry you. Was just trying to let you know Scott is still really pissed."

"About?" I wasn't sure why I was asking this since I had a pretty good idea what he would still be pissed about.

"You know. About you telling the cops about the hidden messages."

"Just how mad was he when you talked to him?"

"Pretty mad. Like, *too* mad, if you ask me."

"And I did."

"And you did what?"

"Ask you."

"Oh yeah. Heh. Right."

"Why did you think he sounded 'too mad'?"

"Because he shouldn't have gotten mad at you for doing the responsible thing. I mean, wouldn't anybody have done what you did by going to the cops with that secret message?"

"I dunno, Seth. If I was one-hundred percent convinced that Scott was innocent, wouldn't I have naturally taken the manuscript to *him* first and shown him the weird message down the left side? Wouldn't I?"

"B-but you do think he's innocent, don't you? Or, don't you?"

I sighed. I was fairly certain that Scott couldn't have killed Charlotte—frankly, I saw no real motive anywhere except for the usual cliché of one spouse killing the other spouse.

Then again, as I kept remembering, that was a cliché for a reason, wasn't it?

"Mom? You still there?"

How long had I been musing silently with this cell phone glued to my ear?

"Yeah, sorry. I was just trying to weigh the pros and cons of assuming Scott is innocent."

"So, you're reducing this to a list of pros and cons now?"

"Yes and no."

He snorted a laugh. "That's totally not helpful, Mom."

"I know. Sorry. I just can't seem to wrap my head around anyone killing Charlotte, so I keep defaulting back to that tried and true assumption that the husband did it."

"Mom, she wrote some weird stuff. Who knows what kind of crazy fans have been out there gunning for her? Plus, what about that website stuff?"

Seth had a point. That cryptic floating message we had found on her website that first day naturally pointed to an insane fan. Or a jealous one. Or some sort of fanatic. I had been subconsciously hoping that Scott hadn't been involved at all, if only for the sake of their son, Teddy, who was far too young to have lost his mother.

"Well, Seth, no matter what I'm currently thinking, I need to call Scott about this second manuscript. I just finished reading it."

"Uh oh. Does it have a secret message or something, too?"

"No, that's the weird thing. None of that stuff at all. In fact, it's just a beautiful story. Haunting. Elegant."

"Wait... no horror? No weird stuff?"

"Nope. None. And I have to tell Scott."

"How do you think he's going to react? I mean, this probably isn't what he expected to hear when he handed you those manuscripts, right?"

"Right. But he needs to know. This might even help him heal a little bit, to know his wife was working on something this... beautiful."

"Is it publishable?"

"Well, it's not finished. But if it were complete, then yes, it would most definitely be worthy enough to be published."

"That's a shame. But yeah, you gotta show it to Scott."

"I'm going to give him a call, even though you said not to contact him."

"Yeah, I think that's best. I didn't know about this new manuscript when I texted you. Definitely contact him. Just make sure it's a phone call first instead of heading right over there."

"Why?"

"Just to be on the safe side, Mom. Geez."

Chapter 22

COULD FEEL MY HEART RACING as the phone rang a second and then a third time. The last interaction I had had with Scott hadn't been an overly pleasant one, and although we had theoretically patched things over a little, we weren't really in positive territory in terms of our relationship. Add on the fact that the man was grieving the loss of his wife—to murder, no less—and I wasn't entirely sure how to approach a phone call as weird as this one was apt to be. But still, it was better than showing up at his door unbidden, stack of papers in hand and news I wasn't sure he was ready to hear.

Somewhere around the fourth ring, while I was starting to think I'd get his voice mail, Scott picked up the phone.

"Hello?"

"Scott, this is Maggie Velam. We... we need to talk."

Silence. That's never good.

Then I heard him sigh loudly. Also never good.

"Listen, Maggie, I understand why you did what you did. Kind of. I'm not sure there's really much we need to talk about at this—"

"Wait! It's not about that first manuscript. I know I should have come to you first, and I apologize again for not doing that. This is about that other manuscript. The second one."

"What about it?"

I could hear the skepticism in his voice. Couldn't say I blamed him. But surely he was also a little bit curious.

"It's… different from the first one."

"So, no top-secret hidden messages in that one?" he asked, dripping with sarcasm. I chalked it up to a lot of crap flying in his direction in the past few weeks and let it go. No need for both of us to get testy.

"No, nothing like that. This second one *is* a story. A real story. A really *good* story, as a matter of fact."

"You don't say?"

"Yes, really. It is. In fact, I was quite moved when I read it. Once I started and realized it was a story and not a coded message, I couldn't put it down. It's that good."

"Huh."

He wasn't saying much, but what he *wasn't* saying was telling me so much more right now. Sometimes the silences spoke volumes.

"You'll want to see this, so I was wondering if I could swing by and drop it off."

"And just why would I want to see this story?"

"Because it's so good. It's not finished—doesn't have a proper ending—but it's mostly there. And it's… beautiful."

"Huh."

"Yes, no exaggeration."

"Beautiful, you say? In what way? I'm not sure I'd use the word 'beautiful' to describe anything my wife used to write."

"I wouldn't either, Scott. But this is completely different from the stuff she was writing and selling. Completely."

"How so? It's not horror or dark fantasy?"

"No, not at all. It's probably more like literary fiction. I keep coming back to the word 'beautiful.'"

"So I hear, yes."

I wasn't sure why it sounded as if he was going to need some real convincing. I would have thought he would have been thrilled, or at least comforted, by the fact that his wife had written something like this, even if she had stuffed it in a drawer. Pretty sure his hesitation had as much to do with not trusting me as it did with what I was actually saying.

"Can I bring it back to you? It belongs to you now."

He sighed again, but this time I had a hunch it was more from emotional exhaustion than annoyance at me.

"Sure. Bring it over. I have no idea what I'm supposed to do with it, but I suppose it should be here."

I heard a tumble of footsteps in the background and then heard his son Teddy's voice bleed into the conversation. I heard Scott thunk the phone down and then picked up some of their conversation.

"No, Teddy, not just now. We can go out in a little bit and play catch."

I heard some whining and then the sound of those same footfalls receding. Scott picked the phone back up.

"Sorry about that. Teddy wanted something."

"No problem. I should keep this short anyway. Is this evening a good time to swing by? I really just need to give this back to you and don't need to stay long."

One final sigh from Scott, a quick "Sure, come on over," and then he clicked to end the call.

Abrupt, but pretty much what I expected. I was going to urge Scott to find a way to get a ghost writer to finish Charlotte's story and have it published under her name. Or, even better, perhaps he could find the file on her computer somehow and see if she had worked on it after printing out the copy I had here. For all I knew, it was already finished—but wasn't part of this stack of pages. I wanted to see Charlotte's name associated with this gorgeous writing, this captivating story. She deserved that much. Even if her husband didn't seem to think so.

Chapter 23

I STEPPED OUT OF MY APARTMENT BUILDING, purse slung precariously over my right shoulder, keys in one hand and the binder-clipped stack of manuscript pages in the other. Out at the curb I spotted Helga's ugly neon green Cube. I had thought that buying a Nissan Cube was already a standout move in any parking lot or situation. But, to spring for the extra bucks to get that hideous custom paint job was beyond my personal level of comprehension.

And yet, it fit Helga and her larger-than-life personality so well, so instead of cringing when I saw it, I usually chuckled and dashed right over. Today was no different. I waved my keys in the air as a makeshift hello as I approached. She lowered her passenger door window and leaned my way.

"Hey, Mags! How ya doin'?"

"Helga, howdy! I didn't expect to see you here! Were we going to have lunch or something and I forgot?" That certainly was not outside the realm of possibility, with the way my mind had been grinding through all the stuff I'd been flinging at it in recent days.

"No, nothing like that. I was just hoping to catch you at home, that's all. Hop in!" She unclicked the lock mechanism for the passenger door and I unhygienically grabbed my keys between my teeth to free up that hand to open the door. Once inside, I dumped the manuscript on my lap, the purse at my feet, and the keys back in my now-empty hand.

"So, you're kidnapping me, or what?"

Helga glanced at the manuscript in my lap. "Were you on your way out then?"

I nodded. "Yup. You literally just caught me. Another five minutes and I would have been gone."

"To… to see… Scott?" Her eyes never left the manuscript on my lap, but she raised an eyebrow in curious questioning.

"Actually, yes. I'm bringing this back to him."

She narrowed her eyes and reached a tentative hand over toward the stack of papers.

"Is this the one with the weird messages in it?"

I shook my head. "No, that's the first one."

"So what's so special about this one? Anything?"

"Actually, yes and no. It's a really lovely story all by itself, but it's not finished. No secret coded messages in it that I could see."

Helga sighed and turned her gaze to the road again. "Then at least let me take you over to Scott's house to drop it off. After we have dinner. Let's hit that steakhouse over by the old railroad depot."

She didn't need to be her usual overly persuasive self to get me to agree to that.

"My GOODNESS, HELGA, if that steak were any rarer, it would be mooing."

"Moo!" she said as she skewered another red, dripping piece of cow flesh and popped it into her mouth. "Just the way I like it. I love this place. They're not afraid to let the cow run right out of the pasture and onto your plate."

I choked on the piece of medium-well steak I had ordered. "Well, that's one way to make it sound, um, appetizing."

She grinned from across the table. "Different strokes, missy."

"Apparently." I scooped up some of the twice-baked potatoes on my plate and let them melt in my mouth before swallowing. My German heritage was showing in my near-worshipful attitude toward these potatoes. I had lived the past year with a newly developed allergy to shellfish, but I wasn't sure I could survive if I were ever diagnosed as allergic to potatoes. "Weird Al" Yankovic's parody song "Addicted to Spuds" was as close to a personal anthem as I was likely to get.

"So, Maggie, once Scott has this literary masterpiece back in his hot little husband hands, what is he going to do with it?"

"Unsure," I said after swallowing the potatoes. "I talked to him on the phone about it, and he seemed less than enthusiastic. He didn't seem at all excited that she had written this beautiful story. If I had to guess, he sounded more like he was worried that a completely different genre with Charlotte's name on it might ruin her reputation as a dark fantasy author."

"Or ruin her *sales*," Helga said, still concentrating on that mooing hunk of beef on her plate.

I stopped chewing and looked over at Helga, who could tell I was looking at her and looked up at me in return.

"What?" she asked.

"What made you say that?"

"Nothing. Just, well, you know. I can't imagine anyone would want to see a big source of passive income like that dry up all of a sudden. Poof! It's gone."

"But it would be a real shame not to see this story in print someday."

"Pen name?" she offered as she chomped on the latest bit of bloody meat.

"Possibly. I'll suggest that to him later if he seems hesitant. I'd hate to think his reticence is just about the money, though."

"A lot of things are just about the money, Maggie. That's life."

She was right. I hated to admit it, but she was often right. "I know. I don't blame him. He's raising a son now on his own. But I'd like to see him find a way to get this out there. Maybe then someday he can come forward to say that it was written by Charlotte."

Helga shook her head before taking a sip of her cabernet. Maybe it was the odd mix of customer noises in the background, but I was sure I heard her slurp. Only Helga could slurp a glass of wine in public and get away with it.

"Don't count on it, sweets. That man might seem like he had no reason to off his cash-cow wife, but weirder things have happened. Weirder things have happened *to you.*" She raised her glass to me as she said this and nodded, before sipping (or slurping) yet again.

Again, she was probably right. In general. Surely Scott could not have *really* killed Charlotte. Not Scott. But then again, without any forced entry to the house and no other real motive, who else could have shot Charlotte in her own home?

Chapter 24

SCOTT PEEKED OUT THROUGH the small beveled-glass window to the right of their front door and then unlocked and opened the door for me.

"Just double-checking that you weren't some kind of wacko fan trying to get in," he said, stepping back and turning to head into the living room. I followed and shut the door behind me, turning the deadbolt with my free hand to lock it again.

"Are you getting harassed?" I asked. It was one part of this whole ugly situation that hadn't really occurred to me, but when someone is married to a famous person, that sort of behavior was probably always on the edges of their lives. It had to be a little more serious with Charlotte gone now.

"Not too much, but you can't be too careful. That thing with the website kinda freaks me out and keeps me on my toes. I especially don't want Teddy to see anything crazy."

We were in the living room and he motioned to the sofa for me to sit down. I nodded and sat, and he took a seat in the large recliner opposite me.

"So, Maggie," he began, pulling the lever on the side of the recliner and yanking the footrest up until it fell into place with a loud click, "what's up with this other manuscript? If it's not another hidden message and we don't need a secret decoder ring or anything, then what gives?"

He sounded suitably skeptical. I had my work cut out for me.

"It needs to be published. Somehow. Some way. It's *that* good."

"You're just a proofreader. How would you know if it's 'that good'?"

"Because I've worked with a lot of other authors. And I'm a reader. I couldn't put it down once I started reading it. And not just because of all the mystery surrounding it. I got lost in this story."

"Lost."

"Yes, lost. And, I still want to read the ending."

"It's not finished? There's no ending?"

"No, not in what I have here. Looks to be about forty thousand words, give or take."

"And how long does it have to be, to be finished?"

"Short novel should probably be over fifty thousand, or closer to sixty."

"What would you call something this long then?"

"Unfinished."

"How do you know it's not finished?"

I tapped a finger on the clipped stack of papers on my lap. "The story drops off a cliff all of a sudden. It's definitely not done. Yet. I think it should be finished, though. By somebody."

"But not *Charlotte*, obviously."

"Unless…" I caught myself before I said too much. I wasn't getting a good vibe from Scott. He had all kinds of guard up trying to keep me out. A fair response, but yet also unfair. I had been forthcoming with him about my reasons for going to the police with the first manuscript. He just still wasn't in a position to see that clearly. Not yet.

He raised an eyebrow. "Unless what?"

"Well, I hate to say."

"Go ahead and say anyway. Please."

He grabbed the footrest lever again and yanked it in the opposite direction. With another loud thud the footrest swooped down and hid inside the bottom of the recliner. Scott sat up straight and then leaned forward. His body language was freaking me out a little bit. I felt the beginnings of a confrontation oozing across the coffee table toward me, and I wasn't sure if it was just my tendency to overthink things, or if he really was trying to intimidate me a little. If it was the latter, it was working.

"Unless the file is somewhere on her computer. You know, with more to the story than this printout."

"I told you I looked for these two files already. Couldn't make heads or tails out of stuff on that cluttered computer of hers. I just stopped looking."

"I… I understand. Maybe you're just not ready yet. But when you are, please do look on her computer some more. Wouldn't you—"

"Wouldn't I what?" he interjected. The sharp tone was unmistakable. I could almost see the chip on his shoulder from here.

"Wouldn't you want to see a wonderful story like this published? With Charlotte's name on it?"

I tried to look as sympathetic and pleading as I could. He needed to do this, for Charlotte. I fought the urge to go to either extreme: looking pathetic instead of sympathetic, like one of those paintings of sad kids with ridiculously huge eyes; or looking menacing and threatening in order to get him to do what I wanted. I think—I hoped—I managed to land somewhere around the midpoint of normalcy: simply trying to express my firm belief that this second manuscript was worth saving, was worth showing to the world.

"I don't know, Maggie," Scott answered finally. "I would have to read it first, to see what it's all about." He was frowning a bit, but it seemed to be the sort of frown that meant he was thinking about it and considering it as a possibility. At least I hoped so.

"Fair enough. That's partly why I brought it back. You need to sit when you have some time to devote to it and read it carefully. Then tell me what you think."

"Do you think it might sell? Like, sell well?"

"Scott, I'm a proofreader, not an agent or publisher. I have no idea what sells these days."

"A few minutes ago you were trying to convince me that it needed to be published, that you work with all these authors, blah blah blah. Now you're just a proofreader?"

"I just know that, as a reader, I appreciated the story and the writing far more than anything Charlotte had been writing up until now. If good, solid literary fiction is selling, then *this* will sell."

"Maybe. We'll see. Maybe I could ask her publisher, then."

I nodded. "Good idea."

"I know the horror stuff sells like crazy, though. With her name on it. I don't wanna damage those sales by putting out something under her name that would confuse her loyal readers. Not now. Not... when we aren't ready to do without her income yet."

I balked at this and hesitated before speaking next. I could tell Scott was walking that ugly tightrope of early grief, and his emotional gait wasn't entirely steady yet.

"Are you guys okay, financially? You and Teddy?"

He made an audible *pffft!* noise and shook his head. "Oh, we're fine, Maggie. Fine. It's just that this was all so unexpected. And, of course, the life insurance is tied up with the investigation."

"How is that progressing? The investigation, I mean." I realized as soon as I said it that it was probably inappropriate, as was asking about their finances. Not that that sort of thing ever really stopped me. Scott frowned but didn't look especially menacing. I think that bothered me more. I sensed a sort of bunched-up restraint in him that I hadn't seen before. Or just hadn't noticed.

"Dunno. The cops won't talk to me."

I heard a small thud or a crash from somewhere else in the house and sucked in a breath.

"Teddy?" Scott called.

"Sorry, Dad!" came the sheepish reply from what I assumed was their home office at the end of the hall.

"Maggie, I have to go see what happened and deal with whatever fallout there is. I hope he didn't break anything valuable."

Just then Teddy himself came dashing into the living room and skidded to a stop on the hardwood floor in his socks. It reminded me a little of the famous Tom Cruise slip-'n-slide moment from *Risky Business*. But at least Teddy was fully clothed.

"Dad, sorry! *Sorry!*" He looked as if he was in full-on panic mode.

"What happened, Teddy?" Scott asked as he stood, towering over his son and putting his hands on his hips.

"I was playing Minecraft on M-Mom's laptop—you said I could, remember?—and I spilled my chocolate milk on—"

"On what? Please tell me you didn't spill it on the laptop, Teddy," Scott said, his voice clipped and his hands now clenched at his sides.

"I'm sorry."

"What have I told you about having food or drinks in that office? Especially with a computer on!"

Scott gave me a quick backwards glance and then turned frontward and started out of the living room. I sensed that this might not be the best time for an extended visit to keep talking about his wife's writing talent and stood up myself. I was feeling generally uncomfortable anyway and thought this was the perfect time to skedaddle.

"Scott, I'll just leave this here for you." I leaned over and gently put the printout on the coffee table. "Take care of whatever spilled and I'll show myself out."

He nodded briskly and then darted out of the living room, with Teddy right behind him. As I walked toward the hallway and the front door, I glanced back and saw Teddy looking back at me as he continued following Scott down the hallway toward their home office, in the opposite direction from me. I smiled weakly, unsure what to say or do for the poor kid.

"Sorry, buddy. Chin up," was all I managed amid my useless smiling. His bottom lip quivered and he nodded, then turned and rounded the corner at the end of the hallway near the door to the office.

I wasn't sure what to make of this whole situation, and now I was left wondering if anybody else had a better motive for murdering Charlotte. Because I was starting to worry that Scott wasn't being completely honest with me about something. I just wasn't sure what it was.

Chapter 25

I WALKED BRISKLY OUT THE DRIVEWAY to Helga's neon green Cube parked on the street. She looked as if she was snoozing behind the wheel so I gently tapped on the passenger window to get her attention. She startled awake, looked over at me, and then started the engine while hitting the Unlock button on her driver's side door. I opened the door and slid in, closing it behind me.

"Sorry that took so long, Helga. You're a champ to wait here for me to get done."

"Ya know," she said, hiding a yawn behind her hand, "I knew you wouldn't be able to just dash on in, drop the papers on the couch, and dash back out."

"Really? How?"

"Because I know you. Once you're in super-sleuth mode, all bets are off. You were probably in there grilling the guy."

"Grilling the guy?"

"You know, giving him the third degree."

"The third degree?"

"You know what I mean."

"Yeah, I know what you mean. But, honest, I wasn't doing that. I was just trying to persuade him to consider finding a way to publish that book."

"So he wasn't too keen on the idea?"

"Not really, no."

"Why not? You said it was really good."

"Oh, it is. He said something about losing her loyal readers."

"Two words for ya, chickie."

"I know."

Together we said, "Pen name."

"I didn't really have time to get into that. His son spilled milk all over his mom's laptop and Scott had to go deal with that. So I let myself out, and here I am."

"Oh yuck."

"I know."

"On his *mom's* computer?"

"Yeah, why? Is that important?"

"Boy, for a nitpicker, you sure can miss some obvious stuff sometimes, Maggie."

"Meaning what, exactly?"

"Didn't you say you hoped Scott would find the story file on her computer, that maybe she'd finished it already but just hadn't printed it all out?"

I let out a sigh and closed my eyes. Of course. I hadn't put those two things together, but Helga was right. Again.

"Oh, shit. Yeah. If Scott can't save that hard drive, then all her files might be lost."

"That's a little bit unnerving. Maybe she backed up her stuff?"

I nodded. "Maybe. I don't know. She wasn't very computer savvy. We might not even get to find out if she had that file on her computer. I don't even want to think about it."

"Sorry, kiddo. I didn't mean to bum you out."

"Consider me bummed out. Time for me to get home. I still have a few freelance projects to get back to. I have even less freelance money coming in than Scott does from Charlotte's books."

"Understatement of the year, I'm sure," said Helga unhelpfully as she put her crazy green Cube in Drive and pulled out onto the street away from Scott and Charlotte's house.

DESPITE MY MORBID CURIOSITY about Charlotte's laptop and the fate of that second story manuscript, I held off contacting Scott the rest of that week. Except for the very next day, to get an update on Charlotte's laptop. Dead as a doornail. I had no idea where that saying originated, but it felt right in this circumstance. The hard drive was baked, and Scott was pretty sure Charlotte never really backed things up. So, if there had been a complete document with the rest of that story on her computer, it was now gone. The bits and bytes were lost. I felt a pang of loss when he told me.

Instead of contacting him any further that week, I caught up on my freelance projects, kept my beak to the grindstone, and invited Seth over for lunch on Saturday. A few days alone with my thoughts had been driving me nuts, and now I had some things I wanted to bounce off Seth, the geek.

"So, you don't necessarily think her site was hacked? By an outsider, I mean?" I asked as he ate.

Seth crunched on a handful of potato chips and shook his head. Reaching for his diet soda, he tried to finish wolfing down the chips so he could talk. I had to remember not to ask him questions while he was fully engaged in a mouthful of food because he clearly could not do those two things at once. Or, perhaps, he simply refused to stop eating long enough to answer my questions. Either way, I was going to end up with spit-out chip crumbs all over my kitchen table if I didn't learn to simply wait it out.

"No," he said once most of the chips were finally down his throat and out of the range of his mouth and vocal cords. "I don't see any evidence of it, really." He was still shaking his head, and he took a healthy swig of the soda and let the bubbles make him blink back tears. He had inherited that weird reaction to carbonated beverages from me, poor kid. My eyes watered terribly any time I grabbed a drink with bubbles. So did his.

"But what about that 'SOMEONE WILL DIE!' thing on the front page of her website? That had to be a hacker, right?" I asked.

"Depends on your definition of a hacker."

"Well, I'm not sure I know my definition of a hacker."

"I mean, it doesn't have to be someone who's heavily into coding."

"Like you?"

"Yeah, like me."

"You know I hate when you do this, right?"

"Do what?" he asked, grabbing another fistful of chips off his plate and stuffing them deftly into his mouth. I marveled at the ease with which he accomplished this. Much better than when he did this stuff at age four or five and slobbered chip crumbs all over his lap.

"When you assume I speak your language. You're going to lose me soon with your computer jargon. You know it's all geek to me." I grinned. He rolled his eyes.

"Mom."

"Sorry. Old joke."

"And yet you still use it."

"Hey, if it ain't broke, don't fix it. Right?"

He grabbed the diet soda and took a healthy slug.

"All I'm saying, Mom, is that I'm starting to think it was just someone who got her password."

"You mean, to her site's blog dashboard?"

"Yeah. It doesn't look like anybody changed any code or anything underneath. The next most logical explanation would be someone with the password."

"Aren't passwords hard to guess, unless you're stupid enough to use obvious ones?"

"Usually, yeah."

"Hmm, wasn't Charlotte a little clueless about online stuff? Maybe her password is something obvious, like her son's birthday. Or her anniversary."

"That's possible." He was frowning, considering.

"But… you don't think that's what happened, do you?"

Now he was shaking his head. "No, I don't."

"Why not?"

"Just a hunch. Because whoever put up the 'SOMEONE WILL DIE!' thing didn't do anything else."

"Well, Charlotte called us and got you over there to help her out right away. Right?"

"There was plenty of time in there for worse things to happen. But pretty much nothing else happened."

"And you changed her password, right?"

"Yeah, she said she didn't remember what it was because her computer just logged her in automatically with cookies. So I got in there and changed it for her."

"To…"

"To something harder to guess. And I wrote it down for her. If you really want to know stuff, I could probably get back in and see when she—or somebody else—had changed things on the site in those days before she died."

"That one day in particular would be helpful, right? The day she called us about it?"

"Yeah."

"Shit."

"What?"

"I didn't tell you yet, but Scott's son spilled milk all over that computer the last time I was there. Earlier this week. It's fried."

"He told you that?"

"Yeah. I talked to him the next day. Gone."

"Maybe I could take a look at it. Milk, you said?"

"Yup. A whole kid's cup full of milk. Right on the laptop keyboard. I left before I got a look at it, but Scott said by the time he got into the office to see what Teddy had done, the milk had seeped down into the keys and the screen was off. He tried turning it upside down and milk kept dripping out for, like, an hour. Then he put the whole thing in a big plastic zipped bag with a bunch of rice."

Seth rolled his eyes. "That's a phone thing. And even then it's iffy. But a whole, wet, milked-soaked laptop? Pretty sure that thing was already dead as a doornail before he ever grabbed that plastic bag." He was shaking his head in apparent disbelief.

"Does it matter that it was chocolate milk?" I offered, grinning. He burst out laughing.

"That probably makes it worse."

"I figured."

"And who doesn't back up their data in this day and age?" He was still shaking his head.

"Charlotte?"

"Charlotte."

"So then, does that mean you can't check her dashboard anymore, since her computer is fried?"

"No, why would it?"

"Because you had to use her computer the first time since she couldn't remember her password."

"No. Because I—"

"Changed the password! Right!"

"And I wrote it down."

"And you still have it?"

"Of course I still have it. I even remember what it is. She was a client. That way I could take a look at things here instead of having to go back over there if she had called me with any other problem."

I nodded. "Right. Right. So, can we log in from here and take a peek?"

"Sure, but what would you be looking for?"

"I dunno. I just don't have very many other ideas."

"About?"

"About who killed Charlotte. The police aren't sharing anything with me, obviously. They're probably still laughing at me bringing the wrong document to them."

Seth snorted. "You gotta admit, Mom. That was pretty classic."

"Oh sure, laugh it up, kiddo."

And he did.

Chapter 26

WE WERE BACK IN MY OFFICE at my main desktop computer. Seth was in my office chair and I had pulled up the overstuffed chair from the other side of the room to sit beside him. He pulled up the main blog site and tried logging in with Charlotte's credentials. Username. Password. Incorrect.

"Huh."

"Try again."

"Duh."

Conversations like this were the glue that held our family together.

Username.

Password.

Incorrect.

"Your keyboard is different from mine. Maybe my finger slipped." He frowned and poised his hands over the home row again, then breathed in deeply.

"You know, if you click on that little eyeball to the right, it'll show you what you're typing," I said.

"Mom."

"What?"

"I know."

"Oh, sorry."

I bit my lip and shut my big fat yap.

Username.

Password. With the little eyeball clicked this time.

2020snillocettolrahc2020

I leaned in a little closer and squinted. "Wait, that's—"

"Yeah, her name backwards. I know it's not the best password, but I meant to give her something better, something randomly generated so it would be virtually impervious."

He hit Enter.

Incorrect.

"Shit!" he blurted out, clearly frustrated.

"Okay, what does that mean?"

"'Shit'? You know what 'shit' means." He smiled, but he was obviously upset.

"I mean, what does it mean that the password isn't working?"

"Obviously it means that *that* isn't the password!" he said, stabbing a finger at the screen right where the incorrect password still sat blinking at him.

"How can that be? You changed it on purpose."

"Obviously someone else changed it after I changed it."

"Obviously," I said, not really feeling it quite as firmly as Seth felt it.

"Shit."

"So you said."

He crossed his arms and sat back in the chair, rolling it around to face me in the armchair. "Charlotte died, what? The day after I changed the password?"

"Something like that, yeah. Why?"

"You knew her better than I did, Mom. Would she have changed the password again after I changed it for her?"

"Well, I didn't really know her online computer habits or skills as well as *you* did," I countered. "But offhand, if she was as clueless as she seemed, then I don't even think she would have known how to change her password. Not easily, anyway."

"That's my guess, too."

He was tapping his foot loudly on my hard plastic chair mat, his arms still crossed against his chest.

"So, what are you thinking? Because it's clear you're thinking something."

He shook his head again. "It's nothing good, that's for sure."

"Meaning? Wait. You don't mean that you think—"

"Oh yes, I do mean that. Probably exactly what you're thinking I'm thinking."

"You mean, you're thinking that—"

"Yup."

"That—"

"Yes! That Scott changed the password."

"Sometime after you changed it."

"Yup."

"Meaning, sometime after Charlotte was killed."

"Yup."

"Why, though? What reason could he have at that point? He was the only adult left in the house."

I stood and walked away from the desk area over to the daybed across the room from my desk. I had to pace this one out. My mind was racing and my feet just wanted to keep moving. On my third circle around the small office, Seth stopped me by putting his arm out across my path.

"Mom, stop. Let's think this through."

"Okay." I sat back down in the armchair and Seth spun the desk chair around to face me.

"What reasons might a newly widowed husband and father have for changing a password on his dead wife's website dashboard?"

I breathed in deeply and held it for a second before blowing it out loudly. "Well, maybe he didn't like your version and changed it to something he could remember more easily."

Seth nodded. "Possible. Possible. But mine was meant to be temporary and so I made it fairly easy to remember. In fact, I'd call it stupid. I was just trying to make things easier for Charlotte that day because we needed to get ahead of that creepy message on her site. I had every intention of walking her through setting up a better one, a more complicated and random one. But I left that for another day because she seemed so… overwhelmed that day."

"And then…"

"Yeah, and then…"

"I think I need to talk to Scott again."

"Mom, is that a good idea?"

"Don't you want to know why he changed the password?"

"I wrote it down on a slip of paper for Charlotte. A sticky note. Maybe Teddy found it and Scott just wanted to change it so Teddy couldn't get into the site."

I nodded. "Possible. Yeah, definitely possible. Especially since we now know that Teddy was allowed to use that laptop."

"So, you don't really need to know exactly why he changed it, do you?" Seth looked worried.

"What's the big deal? I just want to talk to him. Actually, I want to continue our talk about publishing that second manuscript. Asking about the password seems like it'd be a good conversation starter with him." I stood again and started pacing once more.

"Mom. Mom. I know what happens when you get like this. You can't go over there. Not like this."

I stopped pacing and turned to face him. "Not like what, exactly?"

"You'll end up accusing him of something. Blurting something out and getting yourself in trouble."

"What kind of trouble?"

"What if Scott killed Charlotte?"

I looked at Seth and sighed. "Wait, what? Do you really think that?"

"I… miiiight."

"Because of the password?"

"Mayyyybe." He smiled.

"I'll be careful. I'd still have trouble thinking Scott killed his own wife, but I admit something about this whole thing smells funny. I guess I just want to know what's going on. And the only way to find out is to go over there."

"Sometimes I wish you'd act like the introvert I know you are, Mom."

"Of course I'm an introvert. Where do you think you got it from?"

"Not from Dad, that's for sure!"

He stood up and rolled the desk chair off to one side.

"Seth, I'll be careful."

"You keep saying that, which usually means you'll end up in trouble. Just promise me one thing."

"Sure. What?"

"Don't bring Helga along!"

We laughed and fell into a brief but welcome hug. He was probably right about Helga, though. That woman was trouble on wheels.

Chapter 27

HELGA PICKED ME UP about two hours later. I had debated the pros and cons of calling Scott to ask if we could come over, but instead I called Helga and asked her to pick me up so we could go over together. My plan was to have her wait in the car while I went in to talk to Scott. Seth couldn't go with me because he had a meeting with the other folks on his baseball team, the Raging Avocados. They were considering starting back up next season and needed to regroup about player positions and other considerations now that the team was down two people from last year: Allen, who had been murdered, and Frank, my ex-boyfriend, who had been implicated in his murder. I was proud of Seth and the Avocados for getting their act together and boldly moving forward. It had been a rough year for them all.

So, since I wanted someone else to know where I was, I called Helga to alert her. Naturally, this set off her panic-buttons and she insisted that she drive me over there so that I wasn't at Scott's place alone with no backup. I wasn't sure what a woman close to retirement age was going to do to assist me if Scott had murdered his wife. In a theoretical situation like that, he clearly could kill me quickly enough that Helga would be useless sitting out in that green Cube listening to the greatest hits of Herb Alpert and the Tijuana Brass on her phone. Or whatever it was she liked to listen to.

Still, I felt strangely safer knowing Helga would be out there in her silly car waiting for me. So, off we went, two idiotic middle-aged women in the world's most uniquely distinguishable car since the Oscar Mayer Wienermobile.

"I'm not sure how one changed password leads you back into sleuth mode, chickie, but you know I've got your back, right? No matter what."

"Thanks, Helga. I think it's just the better part of wisdom to have a buddy along for stuff like this."

"Right you are!"

We pulled onto Scott's street and then slowed to a stop right in front of his house. His car was in their driveway so I assumed that meant he was home.

"Now, listen, Maggie," Helga said conspiratorially, leaning over and yanking her seatbelt along with her, "just be careful in there, okay? Don't provoke the guy. Find out what you came to find out and then get your ass back out here. If you end up with anything that seems anything like evidence against Scott, we can go to the cops. Okay?"

I nodded. "Okay."

"Promise?" She tugged at my jacket collar.

"Yes, Helga! I promise!" I feigned annoyance but smiled to let her know I would comply. "Seriously, I promise."

"Good. Now, go in there and get 'em."

"You do know that I'm not convinced he really did it, right?"

"Of course you're not. You wouldn't be going in there alone if you were. Right?"

"Right."

"But he knows more than he's telling. Right?"

"Right."

I opened the passenger side car door and took a deep breath before climbing out. Giving Helga a thumbs-up, I turned and strode up the front sidewalk to the door. One press of the doorbell and I stood on the small porch quietly, my heart beating so loudly I was sure Helga could hear it back in her car.

Before I had a chance to overthink why I was standing on Scott Collins's front porch, the door swung open and there was Scott, staring at me from behind the storm door. He hesitated before opening the door. I probably looked suitably sheepish at the intrusion, but I was certain I felt twice as awkward as I looked.

"What do you want?" he asked bluntly. He looked as if he hadn't slept in a week. Hair sticking up all over his head, at least a two-day growth of stubble across his face, wrinkles on his T-shirt that indicated he had probably slept in it at least once.

"Just to… well, can we talk? About the book?"

"That new one? The printout?" He ran one hand across his chest, scratching an itch absentmindedly, and squinted against the mid-afternoon sun streaming across his face.

"Yes, that one. May I…? Can we talk about it?"

He had this look on his face that worried me. Was he going to slam the door in my face, or would he relent and let me in?

"Come in," he said, his voice soaked with reluctance and an odd sort of surrender. He held the storm door open wider and I stepped past him into the front foyer. I turned to see him glance out to the street, registering Helga's car as one he'd seen before.

"Is that your… friend? What's her name? Olga?"

"Helga. Yeah, she drove me over today."

"Oh, uh…"

"We're… going to dinner after this. Figured it was easier to just merge the two trips. I won't stay long."

He visibly relaxed at that. It was clear he hadn't wanted company. As an introvert, I had to empathize with that perspective. I never liked unannounced visitors, either.

The door closed and we were standing in the foyer. He made no move to, well, move, and I got the distinct impression he wanted to have this conversation here in the foyer. The message was clear.

"I'm just trying to convince you to show that manuscript to her agent. It's worth something. It's worth pursuing."

"So you keep saying."

"You don't agree?"

"Maggie, listen. The one thing I know about Charlotte's readers is that they're immature and fickle. Throwing a completely different book into her backlist could jeopardize the fragile hold she still has on them."

"From here it looks like her sales have skyrocketed since her—since she—"

"Since she died."

"Yes."

"I suppose. And I want to keep it that way. Readers in her genre are wackos to begin with, let's face it. I don't want to do anything that might alienate them." He let out a sigh and scratched across his chest again, using his other hand to run through his hair, trying to tame it a little. To no avail, though I neglected to mention this.

"Helga and I thought maybe a pen name might work. Maybe discuss that with her agent."

"You said yourself that the story isn't even finished. Why should I give her agent an unfinished manuscript?"

"Have you read it yet?"

"No," he said quietly. "I just don't have it in me, Maggie. I'll take your word for it that it's, what did you call it? Beautiful?"

"It's all sorts of things, Scott. Beautiful. Elegant. Lovely. Marvelous. It has potential."

He closed his eyes, shook his head, and was silent. I felt I was fighting an uphill battle. I wasn't sure whether I was crossing a line yet or not, so I refrained from continuing and let him gather his thoughts.

"I don't think so, Maggie. If she ever finished it, it would have been on the laptop. And everything on that laptop is gone now."

"There are ghost writers out there, Scott. People who could mimic her writing style in that book and finish it for her. You didn't find anything else in that desk, did you?"

"Such as?"

"Maybe an outline for the story? Notes?"

He shook his head and folded his arms across his chest. "Nope. Nothing like that. Sorry."

I wasn't sure why he felt he had to apologize to me for that. It would affect him a lot more than me.

"Speaking of the computer, I have a question for you. From, well, from Seth."

He looked at me, frowning. "Seth?"

"Yeah. He tried to get into Charlotte's blog dashboard again today, but he said somebody changed the password to get in."

"Didn't he change the password? That day the weird message showed up?" He was still frowning.

I nodded. "Yeah, he did. But he said that new one wasn't working. Now, in theory Charlotte could have changed it to something else after Seth left that day, but that was only, like, a day or so before she was… was…"

"Murdered."

"Yeah," I said softly. I hated hearing it. "And she wasn't very tech savvy, according to Seth."

"It wasn't me, if that's what you're asking. Why would I want to change her password after she was dead?"

I shook my head. "We couldn't think of any reason why either of you would want to change it."

"Well, sorry I can't help you with this, either." He turned to look at the clock on the wall in the foyer. "Look at the time. Hey, I gotta get ready to take Teddy to his soccer game. We're gonna have to cut this short. I wish I had better things to say, but I'm at a loss for words. About the book and about the password. Sorry."

He gestured to the door right behind me, and I got the hint. Time to skedaddle.

"I understand. Really, I do. I just wish I knew what to say to change your mind."

"Maybe ask me again in a year, after things around here have settled down."

He had a point. Maybe it was all still too fresh. Time might give us both a better perspective. I opened the door just as I heard a cell phone ring distantly behind me, somewhere else in the house. I turned to face Scott again.

"Look, I gotta answer that," Scott said and shrugged.

"Go, yes. Go answer it. I'll close the door behind me."

He dashed away, down the hall toward the office. As I started to turn again toward the door, I saw Teddy running toward me from the living room. If he'd been in there the whole time, then he'd been really quiet.

"Miss Maggie!" he said in a low, quiet tone unusual for a boy his age.

"Yes?"

Teddy looked around furtively and then sidled up closer to me so that he could speak more quietly.

"My dad."

"Yes? What about your dad?"

"I think he hurt my mom."

My heart skipped a beat. "Hurt her? When?"

"That day. That. Day."

I bit my lip and kept myself from showing everything I was feeling.

"What do you mean, hurt her?"

"I… don't know. It's all blurry to me. I was upstairs playing Fortnite. I had the headphones on because I'm not allowed to play games on a school day. So I had my door closed, too. Then I heard this boom sort of noise and took the headphones off."

I hated to think Teddy had seen anything that fateful day. I wasn't sure what to say or ask him right now, but I had to know.

"What happened next? Did you… go downstairs?"

"No! I heard my dad running around downstairs and figured they were fighting or something. So I stayed upstairs where it was quieter."

I nodded, touched his forearm, and said nothing. He wanted to talk. I let him.

"I got scared and put the headphones back on. I figured if one of them dropped something or broke something, I'd find out about it later. I don't like when they fight."

"Nobody likes that, do they? When their parents fight."

He shook his head, and I noticed his bottom lip quivering. I wanted to dash out the door to Helga's car and go get the police, but I couldn't just leave Teddy here with his dad. Not with what I was now thinking about what happened that day.

"By the time I got brave enough to take the headphones back off, I could hear tons of people downstairs. You know, the police. The ambulance."

"Teddy?"

Both Teddy and I looked up to see Scott standing in the foyer with us. We both froze and said nothing. My heart was in my throat but I had nowhere to go without endangering myself or, worse, Teddy.

"Dad?" he croaked.

"What are you telling Maggie?"

"N-nothing."

"It didn't sound like nothing."

I had to speak up.

"Scott, what did you hear? He didn't say anything much. Just about how he felt th-that day." Great. I was stuttering. It was abundantly clear I was scared out of my wits. I really had to work on that someday.

"Listen, Maggie, it's not what you think."

"What I think? I, I don't think anything."

"Sure you do. You were probably thinking it when you came in the door. And then Teddy came out and fed into your fear. I can practically see it from over here. It's all over your face."

"It is? What is?" I was fumbling badly. I had been wise to skip that acting major in college.

"Maggie, calm down. I'm..." He hesitated, sighing and looking at the floor. He was going to choose his words carefully. "I'm not a murderer."

That wasn't what I had expected to hear. "You're... wait, what?"

He snorted a sarcastic laugh. "Yeah, just as I suspected. You're standing there thinking I killed Charlotte. Me! Her husband."

"Scott, I don't mean to—"

"No, of course you don't. You're just another member of the Husband Did It Club. I hate all of you people. Her fans. The police. Half the people at Teddy's school. The other parents on the soccer team. Everybody. Every single one of you."

"Scott, I really didn't mean to—"

"No, right. Nobody ever means to. And now you're standing here ready to lure my own son into the club. Hell, he was halfway there already, right? You were just here to snag him all the way in. Great."

"No, Scott, no! But, the things he said—"

"Yeah, right. Maggie, we need to talk. Teddy? You need to go upstairs. Go ahead and play Fortnite. I don't mind. And put on those headphones."

He looked up at his dad pleadingly, and I think I had never felt so sorry for a kid before in my life. Sorrier than I even felt for myself at the moment.

"Dad?"

"Teddy, you heard me." Scott pointed at the staircase at the left edge of the foyer.

"Miss Maggie?" Teddy said, turning to look at me with eyes that were going to make me crumble in a minute. Scott looked at me, clearly wanting me to show unity with him, and nodded subtly. I was torn between not wanting to leave myself alone with Scott and not wanting to keep Teddy down here where he was clearly in danger.

"T-Teddy, it's okay. Your dad and I j-just need to talk. Go upstairs. We'll be right down here." I nodded to him, seeing Scott also nodding in my peripheral vision.

Teddy gave us each one last glance, then turned and dashed up the steps without looking behind him. I heard what I assumed was his bedroom door close, and I let out the breath I'd been holding.

Scott and I were alone.

Chapter 28

MAGGIE, IT'S NOT ANYTHING LIKE what you must be thinking."

"Well, I suppose you do know what I'm thinking then." At least I wasn't stuttering. For now.

"I swear to you, I didn't kill Charlotte."

"Then who did?"

"Nobody."

I balked. Had he just said nobody had killed Charlotte? That made no sense.

"What do you mean? She's dead. Isn't she?"

He sighed, nodding. I thought maybe I saw tears welling up in his eyes, but for all I knew he was just a far better actor than I would ever be. I kept my guard up. And I wondered whether Helga could see us standing in the foyer. What body language could I use to signal to her to alert the police? Something that wouldn't give me away to Scott? I blanked.

"Yes, she's dead. That's not quite what I meant."

"Then... what?"

"She wasn't murdered."

"What? Scott, she was shot. In her office."

"Yes, she was."

"How is that not murder?"

He closed his eyes and drew in a long, quivering breath. "When... when she's the only one in the room."

"Wait... what?"

"You heard me. Don't make me say it out loud. I haven't said it out loud to anyone. Even to myself."

"Are you saying she—"

"Yes," he said, cutting me off before I said it.

"That's impossible."

"No, it's very possible. It happened. I was there."

"I was down the hall there, just outside her office."

"You... saw her do it?"

He nodded, now with his lip quivering and tears spilling down his cheeks. I stood rooted to my spot in the foyer near the storm door. My knees were shaking, and I was concerned that I wouldn't be able to stay standing without leaning on something nearby.

"But why?" I was nothing but a bunch of short, clipped questions. I felt so helpless.

"She wasn't happy."

"With... what? Who? You?"

He shook his head. "No, she apologized to me right before she—you know. She wasn't happy about her c-career."

"But she was ridiculously popular. And talented. I always told her that, after every single book. Every. Single. Book. Talented. So... talented." My voice trailed off and I felt tears coming to my own eyes.

"She wouldn't have believed you."

"Wait... this doesn't make any sense. None. She was shot through the heart."

"I know. I think she did that on purpose."

"Why?"

"She didn't want it to look like a suicide. She begged me."

"Begged you to do what?" My brain wasn't wrapping itself around any of this.

"To cover it up. To not let anybody know. I tried. I shooed Teddy back upstairs when I realized he'd heard something. He told me later that Charlotte had been the one to suggest he go upstairs and play Fortnite with the headphones. He loved that because we hardly ever let him play it and never during the week."

"He-he told me he was playing without permission."

"That's what I told him to tell the police. It was horrible to ask that of him."

"You're damned right it was horrible. Why would you get him involved in this?"

"It was the only way I could think of to keep him out of this. If he had told the police that his mom had told him to go upstairs and do something that he wasn't ever allowed to do, well, they would have figured out that she was planning to kill herself."

My mind was still reeling, but pieces were slowly falling into place. "But wouldn't the police be able to tell it was a suicide right away by where the gun was?"

"I moved it. I threw it onto the floor."

"You what?"

"I had to. I was trying not to scream, trying not to throw up. I panicked. I had to keep the police from telling the world my Charlotte had killed herself! You've gotta see that, right? It's an awful thing, and I didn't want Teddy to know that about his mom, either."

Scott shuffled to the wall near the clock and leaned against it. It looked as if he was shivering, though it was plenty warm in the house. My knees were still shaking, and I thought maybe I was going to need a wall to lean on soon, too.

"But... what did the police think then?"

"They know the gun is ours. I fed them the possibility of someone having gotten in the house and then using our gun. I let them think we kept it loaded in her desk drawer."

I was stunned. "Why would you keep a loaded gun in a desk with a nine-year-old in the house?"

Scott was angry. "We didn't! I told the police we did so they'd buy the story about someone getting in and using our own gun."

"That's horrible."

"To me it was better that they think we were irresponsible than think Charlotte had killed herself. I was okay with taking that hit, that stigma or whatever."

His eyes were closed now, and I could see he was trying hard not to relive that scene in his mind. I suspected he was failing miserably.

"What... but what about...?" I could barely piece together my own thoughts, let alone phrase them in a coherent question.

"About what, Maggie?"

"What about the website? Was that message just a coincidence?"

"No, it wasn't."

"But then, who?"

"Charlotte."

"Charlotte what?"

"She put it there."

I coughed out a dry laugh. "Charlotte? She couldn't manage her own blog and passwords, let alone put a message across the front of her website like that!"

"Yes, she could," Scott said quietly, nodding and avoiding eye contact with me. Instead, he looked down at the tiled foyer floor and scuffed one foot along the lines between two of the tiled near him.

"She could?" I was parroting everything he was saying now, just to keep myself from losing my mind.

"Oh yes. She was quite computer savvy, our Charlotte."

I was speechless, which was probably a good thing at this point. But, things were starting to fall into place. Charlotte seeming to forget how to do things with her website and needing more help from Seth. Charlotte always needing praise from me and others that her writing was any good at all. And, most recently, Charlotte's hidden message in that first manuscript.

"Scott," I said quietly. "That manuscript with the hidden message..."

He winced. "Yeah, about that."

"Did you know about the message when you handed me the manuscripts? You didn't, did you?"

He shook his head vigorously. "No, of course not. If I had known about the messages, I would have just burned that manuscript. I certainly wouldn't have given it to a proofreader with an eye for detail."

"No, of course not."

"What better way to point right to suicide than that message?"

"Well, to be honest, I thought it pointed to an unhappy marriage. And then—"

"To me."

I nodded.

"I hadn't even thought of that angle."

"I assumed you had, since you were so mad at me for showing it to the police."

"I was mad because I was sure the cops would declare it a suicide and ruin everything. It was consuming me, worrying that somebody was going to find out."

"Wait, so why the website message then?"

"To make people think she was murdered. She'd been planning to do this for a while. I hadn't pieced it all together and thought it was just a publicity stunt or something for the new book."

Another piece fell into place.

"I think Teddy thinks you killed Charlotte."

Scott nodded. "Yeah, I can see that now. That's not good."

"That's worse than not good, Scott. He must be terrified of you. You need to make this right. It'll hurt him, but at least you and he can have a loving relationship again. He'll have you to help him come to terms with what really happened."

He was still nodding. Pieces were falling into place for him, too. "I know. I know. But it's worse than that."

"How?" I wasn't sure I wanted to hear any more details.

"The laptop? With the chocolate milk?"

"Yes?"

"I told Teddy to do that."

"What?"

"I told him we needed to get rid of everything on his mom's

computer so that the bad people who had hurt her couldn't get into it and change things anymore. He knows just enough about computers and how websites are made to have believed me. So we came up with the idea of him spilling chocolate milk all over it."

"While I was here to be a witness."

"Yes," he said, nodding again. "I'm sorry I got you involved. But I was sure the cops were going to want that laptop at some point. I'm surprised they haven't taken it yet. I know they've been looking at me funny for a while now."

I nodded. "I'm sure they have. I doubt they could come up with any other good suspects because there hadn't been any forced entry. And I didn't realize it was your gun, but they know that, right?"

"Yeah, they do. Boy, did I get a lecture about loaded guns in the house. I just cried a lot—I couldn't help it, knowing what I knew—and they took the gun."

"What about, you know, gunpowder residue and stuff? She would have had that on her hand, right?"

"I wiped it off as best I could."

"I'm pretty sure they'd still be able to tell."

"Probably. They won't tell me anything about the investigation or what they're thinking, but I tell you, I spend most days just wondering when they'll come knocking at my door."

At that exact moment, as if on cue, a loud knocking came from behind me, followed by the door being yanked open forcibly. Three uniformed officers, with guns held in that menacing position at eye level, stormed into the foyer. Both Scott and I instinctively raised both our hands, and I tried to look as wide-eyed innocent as I could. Scott was behind me, and I kept my eyes facing the officers and let him fend for himself. I'd heard enough for one day and was glad not to have to hear any more of his freaky story.

"Scott Collins?"

"Yes, that's me," he said faintly behind me. "This is Maggie Velam. She had nothing to do with this."

The officer slowly moved toward Scott, and I panicked. "Wait!" I yelled. "He didn't do it! Charlotte killed herself! Scott just lost his nerve and covered it up to make it look like a murder!"

The officers all stood still, silent, and then I heard a small voice from somewhere behind me.

"Dad? Is it true?" squeaked Teddy from the landing. I kept my hands raised but slowly turned to see Teddy standing there, a pair of wireless headphones clutched in both hands.

"Teddy, what are you doing there?" Scott asked.

"I got scared for Miss Maggie. I called 9-1-1."

Then, before the officers could do anything about it, Teddy had leapt down the rest of the stairs from that midway point on the landing and had thrown himself into his father's arms. Scott slowly lowered his arms and grabbed his son, hugging him fiercely. They both began sobbing uncontrollably, and I joined them a moment or two later.

I stole a glance at one of the officers—it was the one who had been nice to me the day I dropped off the wrong manuscript—and I was pretty sure I saw a tear slip down his cheek as he stoically held his gun up high and then let it come down slowly. The other two officers followed suit.

I looked past them, out the front door, and saw Helga, now standing outside her puke-green Cube and staring at the spectacle of two police cars in the driveway, lights spinning red and blue. I cautiously waved, hoping she could see me, and I got a half-hearted wave in return.

I was right. Hanging out with that woman was always some kind of trouble.

Chapter 29

FEEL LIKE AN IDIOT BECAUSE I couldn't figure that out for myself," Seth said as he, Annie, and I sat around my kitchen table a week or so later, playing a game of Scrabble. Annie was home for fall break. And Seth was trying to distract us from the fact that he wanted to play another proper noun: UNIX.

"You can't use that word, Seth!" Annie argued as he laid the tiles down on the board. "And you know the rule about using a nerd-word! Not fair."

"Unix! That is so a real word!"

Methought the boy protesteth too much.

"Use it in a sentence then—one that doesn't involve computer jargon."

"Um, how about this? In *Game of Thrones*, the Unsullied army was full of unix."

I burst out laughing, and Annie just swiped at Seth's arm and pouted in an exaggerated manner. Seth joined me in laughing.

"That's *eunuchs*, not Unix!"

"They sound the same to me," Seth said. "Alternate spelling?"

I stood and padded across the room to get more pretzels and

to grab the pitcher of lemonade in the fridge, keeping an eye on my kids because I loved watching them harass each other during our game nights.

Annie shook her head. "Nice try, idiot."

Seth picked up the tiles and shrugged. "That would have been a lot of points, too."

"Try winning without cheating one of these days, would ya?"

"Never."

"Mom?" Annie said, turning to me. "Do you have any more dip?" She raised the bowl and I saw that it was, indeed, empty.

"Sure. Hand it over." She handed me the bowl and I opened the fridge again to get the container of French onion dip. As I was spooning more into the bowl, Seth sighed exaggeratedly.

"Mom?"

"Yeah, Seth?"

"Am I slipping?"

"Slipping? How?"

"Well, I couldn't figure out why there was no real hacker in Charlotte's website."

"Seth, none of us saw it. How could we? We were all convinced it was someone outside the family who'd killed Charlotte."

I licked the last of the dip off the spoon and dumped it in the sink, then clapped the plastic lid back on the dip container and popped it back into the fridge. I turned around to see Seth frowning. He was obviously bummed.

"And I couldn't tell that Charlotte was faking her stupidity about online stuff. How did I not see *that*? She used to know so much more, and then what? She suddenly forgot it? That makes no sense. I should have seen that."

"Seth, that had nothing to do with your skills as a web geek. Nothing. That had more to do with human nature. Being a good judge of character."

"So you're saying I'm a *bad* judge of character?"

I furrowed my brows and pursed my lips. He was really straining at this. "No, not at all. You barely knew Charlotte. As a person, I mean. You only knew her as a client. And remember, you only knew what she chose to show you. If anybody should have noticed it, that would have been me, not you."

I sat back down and put the dip on the table between Seth and Annie. Annie already had a pretzel poised in her hand and scooped up some dip almost as soon as the bowl hit the table. Seth, usually ready to fight Annie over any food I put on the table, was instead sitting back against the kitchen chair, his arms folded across his chest.

"Maybe, Mom. But I still feel a little bit responsible."

"Seth, you're going to have to let this go. I don't think any of us could have stopped her. She'd been planning it for days, weeks. Maybe longer. It's bad enough Scott and Teddy will have to deal with what they think they should have known. Let's not add ourselves to that list of self-imposed guilt, okay?"

Annie reached her free hand across the table and held it open, palm up. Seth looked at it blankly for a moment and then uncrossed his arms and put his hand in hers. She squeezed it and gave him a sweet smile, and my heart squeezed as I watched my kids bonding, Annie helping her brother in a strong, silent show of comfort.

"Seth?" she said softly, blinking.

"Yeah?" he answered just as softly. My heart was going to burst with pride and love.

"Give back that 'Z' tile you stole from Mom's rack while she was getting more dip."

THE END

ABOUT THE AUTHOR

IN THE EARLY 1980S, Linda pursued a writing degree from Carnegie Mellon University in Pittsburgh, Pa. She pursued it but it kept getting away.

She has since worked behind the scenes in publishing as a proofreader, typesetter, and copyeditor. She's worked with publishers, big and small, and with individual authors, big and small. (The big ones really ought to get a little more exercise.) She's also an 8th grade composition coach for WriteAtHome.com.

Linda is currently on the board of the St. Davids Christian Writers' Association and also serves as author liaison for Beaver County BookFest in Pennsylvania. She enjoys comedy, computer gadgets, office supplies, reading, movies, adventure games, crocheting—and her office guinea pigs, who keep her company while she's working.

Her favorite writing challenge since 2004 has been the yearly contest known as National Novel Writing Month: writing 50,000 words of a single new fiction project during the month of November. She loves the pressure of a ridiculous, forced deadline. *Charlotte's Website* started out as a NaNoWriMo novel in 2016.

Linda currently lives in western Pennsylvania with her husband, Wayne Parker. They share six children between them, all of them now grown and living their own humorous stories.

Visit Linda online:
www.lindaau.com

Follow Linda on Twitter:
@LindaMAu

Stalk Linda on Facebook:
Group: www.facebook.com/groups/lindamau
Page: www.facebook.com/AuthorLindaMAu

Look at Linda's stuff on Instagram:
www.instagram.com/austruck1